Libretto for

FRENCH'S MUSICAL LIBRARY

Little Mary Sunshine

book, lyrics and music,
by
Rick Besoyan

SAMUEL FRENCH, INC.

Founded 1830

45 WEST 25th STREET, NEW YORK, N.Y. 10010

It is in violation of the international copyright laws and the laws of the United States of America to copy or reproduce this material by any means whatsoever, anywhere throughout the world.

Amateurs wishing to arrange for the production of LITTLE MARY SUNSHINE must make application to SAMUEL FRENCH, INC., at 45 West 25th Street, New York, N.Y. 10010, giving the following particulars:

(1) The name of the town and theatre or hall in which it is proposed to give the production.

(2) The maximum seating capacity of the theatre or hall.

(3) Scale of ticket prices.

(4) The number of performances it is intended to give, and the dates thereof.

Upon receipt of these particulars SAMUEL FRENCH, INC., will quote the terms upon which permission for performances will be granted.

A standard rental package, consisting of
Piano/Conductor's Score
Flute
Oboe
Bassoon
Clarinet I
Clarinet II
Trumpets I & II (2 Books)
French Horn I & II
Trombone
Percussion
Violins I & II (2 Books)
Viola
Cello
Bass
Harp
Alternative duo-piano arrangement also available
23 Chorus Books
will be loaned two months prior to the production ONLY on receipt of the royalty quoted for all performances, the rental fee and a refundable deposit. The deposit will be refunded on the safe return to SAMUEL FRENCH, INC., of all material loaned for the production.

Stock royalty quoted on application to SAMUEL FRENCH, INC.

Vocal scores are available for $30.00 a copy plus postage.

ISBN: 0573-68084-1

DRAMATIS PERSONAE

(In The Order In Which They Appear)

CHIEF BROWN BEAR   (Chief of the Kadota Indians)

CPL. "BILLY" JESTER (A Forest Ranger)

CAPT. "BIG JIM" WARINGTON (Captain of the Forest Rangers)

"LITTLE MARY SUNSHINE" (MARY POTTS) (Proprietress of the Colorado Inn)

MME. ERNESTINE VON LIEBEDICH (An Opera Singer)

NANCY TWINKLE (Little Mary's Maid)

FLEET FOOT (An Indian Guide)

YELLOW FEATHER (Chief Brown Bear's Son)

GEN. OSCAR FAIRFAX, RET. (A Washington Diplomat)

* * * * *

YOUNG LADIES FROM THE EASTCHESTER FINISHING SCHOOL — CORA, HENRIETTA, GWENDOLYN, BLANCHE, MAUD and MABEL

YOUNG GENTLEMEN OF THE UNITED STATES FOREST RANGERS — PETE, SLIM, TEX, BUSTER, HANK and TOM

Time: Early in this Century

Place: The Colorado Inn, high in the Rocky Mountains

ACT I

A Summer Afternoon

Scene 1:   In Front of the Colorado Inn

Scene 2:   The Garden

Scene 3:   The Inn

Scene 4:   The Primrose Path

Scene 5:   The Inn

ACT II

That Evening

Scene 1:   The Inn

Scene 2:   Point Look-Out

Scene 3:   In Front of Chief Brown Bear's Teepee

Scene 4:   Cora's Bedroom

Scene 5:   The Primrose Path

Scene 6:   Point Look-Out

Scene 7:   The Inn

Scenic Notes

At its simplest, LITTLE MARY SUNSHINE can be a one set-one drop production. The main set should be the exterior of the Colorado Inn; the drop either Point Look-Out or the Primrose Path. The Teepee scene can be played in front of the drop with a simple Teepee cut-out. The bedroom scene can be played on the large set by omitting Blanche's line, "Why don't you go out the front door?" and having Nancy exit and change costume behind a tree Down Left. If swings are impractical, the Swinging number may be omitted. (See piano score for music cut.)

NOTE

It is absolutely essential to the success of the musical that it should be played with the most warmhearted earnestness. There should be no exaggeration in costume, makeup or demeanor; and the characters, one and all, should appear to believe, throughout, in the perfect sincerity of their words and actions.

PROLOGUE*

As the house lights dim a spotlight picks up a YOUNG LADY standing in front of the curtain. She carries a long taper. As she lights the taper she says:

YOUNG LADY

Hello:
(Moving across the stage, she simulates lighting the old-fashioned foot-lights, one by one, while saying:)

I'd like to take you back to a time when the world was much more simple than ours is today. For instance, good meant good, bad meant bad, virtue was all and justice, well, justice always triumphed; at least we like to think it was that way. But before we begin, the company wishes to express its appreciation to everyone who made this production possible, especially,
(Checking notes)
Johann Strauss, Rudolf Friml and Victor Herbert. And now, it gives us great pleasure to present a saga of Colorado —

"LITTLE MARY SUNSHINE"

* Prologue optional.

Act I

SCENE 1

The lights come up and the curtain rises on the exterior of the Colorado Inn. The Inn itself is L. of C., at an angle so that the porch is plainly visible. A rough-hewn sign with the name of the Inn hangs UCR. The entire back-drop is an inspiring view of the snow-capped Rocky Mountains. A large tree stands UR of center.

The curtain music has a feeling of alerted serenity. At curtain CHIEF BROWN BEAR, dressed in a colorful Indian Chief outfit, is discovered UC., standing with one foot on a tree stump. He stands in a "cigar store Indian" pose, looking off R. At break in music he slowly turns front and speaks:

CHIEF BROWN BEAR

(In stilted Indian manner)

Someone come.

(He turns and looks off R. as the music builds. He turns front again)

Forest Rangers come. Me tell Merry Sunshine Forest Rangers come.

(He starts to exit UR., turns and raises an arm above him)

Ka-do-ta!

(CHIEF BROWN BEAR exits U.R.)

> *(Forest Ranger entrance music begins, softly at first; growing louder until the Gentlemen of the Ensemble, THE FOREST RANGERS, enter from U.R., whistling. They march across the stage until they are spread from D.L. to D.R. They are dressed in snappy red uni-forms. The uniforms are complete with hat, gloves and shoulder pack. They are led by CORPORAL "BILLY" JESTER. Billy is our character juvenile; a tenor or high baritone)*

BILLY

(In time to march music)

> *(CAPTAIN "BIG JIM" WARINGTON enters R. Captain Jim is a typical operetta leading man with a strong baritone voice. CAPTAIN JIM crosses to Billy. They salute. BILLY joins ranks as CAPTAIN JIM turns front and begins to sing:)*

THE FOREST RANGER
(CAPTAIN JIM and THE FOREST RANGERS)

CAPT. JIM	We've marched from the Canada border
	To the Mexican border and back
	Returning the lawless to order
	And protecting the weak from attack
	We set a fine example
	Returning good for ill
	Our work is more than ample
	For there's always one more hill
	Beyond a hill
JIM & BILLY	Beyond a hill
TENORS	Beyond a hill
BARITONES	Beyond a hill
ALL	Beyond a hill

— 1 —

CAPT. JIM
& RANGERS
	Stout-hearted is the Forest Ranger
	    He's a scout:
	He's thoughtful, friendly, courteous and kind,
	    He's reverent and grave
	    He's healthy and he's brave
	He's clean in soul and body and mind
	    Yes, Sir!
	He's cheerful, honest, thrifty and obedient
	    To love the good and hate the bad is
	        his plan
	So if there's any danger
	You can be sure the Forest Ranger
	    Ever will march on man to man.

CAPT. JIM	The lonely coyote in the prairie
	    Isn't very tough to us
	The grizzly bear in his lair he
	    Isn't very rough to us
	We've nerves made of steel
	    Bodies of iron
	So please don't estrange
	The Forest Ranger
	    For he's quite magnificent;
	Stout-hearted is the Forest Ranger
	    He's a scout
	He's thoughful, friendly, courteous and kind,
	    He's reverent and grave,
	    He's healthy and he's brave
	He's clean in soul and body and mind
	    Yes, Sir!
	He's cheerful, honest, thrifty and obedient;
	To love the good and hate the bad is his plan
	    So if there's any danger
	    You can be sure the Forest Ranger
	Ever will march on man to man
	To man to man to man to man.

(Dialogue after song)

CAPTAIN JIM

At ease, Gentlemen.

(Xing U.L. to Inn steps)

Gentlemen, I'm afraid I have a piece of disappointing news, for since I sent Sergeant McGinty back to headquarters, against his will I might add, I know how sorely you have missed his kind ministrations. I have just received word, via carrier pigeon, that your beloved top sergeant will be unable to rejoin the outfit for quite sometime for he is suffering from badly strained vocal cords.

(Xing D.C.)

During his absence, Corporal Jester will remain second-in-charge. Corporal!

BILLY

(XXing C. to Capt. Jim, he salutes)

Yes, Sir?

CAPTAIN JIM

Have you been studying your Book of Rules and Regulations, Corporal?

BILLY

Oh, yes, Sir. It's my constant companion, Sir.

CAPTAIN JIM

Good. The Book of Rules and Regulations is the finest companion a Forest Ranger ever had.

BILLY

Oh, yes, Sir. Indeed it is, Sir.

CHIEF BROWN BEAR

And now, Corporal, take command of the troop whilst I make billeting arrangements.

BILLY

Yes, Sir. Thank you, Sir. Troop 'tention! Salute, one!
(CAPTAIN JIM marches into the Inn)
Ho!
(Xing D.R. and turning front so the Forest Rangers can't see him BILLY takes out his Book of Rules and Regulations and hastily thumbs through it. He reads:)
"When taking over command of your troop, let the men know that they can depend on your courageous behavior."
(Xing L., he tosses hat, gloves and pack OFF-STAGE L. while saying:)
At ease, gentlemen. Whilst Captain Warington is away, I'd like to talk to you a little bit about courage.
(Xing D.R.)
Now, courage is vitally important to a Forest Ranger, for courage is something that a man must have here, in his heart, if he is to lead others.
(Unobserved by BILLY, CHIEF BROWN BEAR enters U.R., crosses D.C. walking through the center of the Forest Ranger ranks. The FOREST RANGERS break ranks to observe Chief Brown Bear as BILLY continues:)
Take me, for example: by all outward appearances it might seem that I am not the courageous type, but here,
(Touches heart)
here, where it really counts, there's courage; courage to spare; and I'd like to prove it to you.

CHIEF BROWN BEAR

(Raising an arm)
HOW!

BILLY

(Still oblivious of Chief Brown Bear's presence)
How? You ask me how? Unfortunately, at the moment, there doesn't seem to be any way I can prove my statement, however, if there were, I feel sure that you,
(Turning he sees Chief Brown Bear)
you . . . you?

CHIEF BROWN BEAR

How! Me Chief Brown Bear.

BILLY

(Backing away)
Chief, Brown Bear. I see. Excuse me one moment, Chief.
(Xing D.R. He reads again from The Book of Rules and Regulations)
"Consider all Indians friendly unless mortally assaulted."
(Xing back to CHIEF BROWN BEAR HE shakes the CHIEF'S hand violently)
Very happy to meet you Chief Brown Bear. Very happy, indeed. Have you fellows all met Brown?

— 3 —

CHIEF BROWN BEAR

Me Chief of Kadota Indians. Peace! Me bring peace from Kadota Indians to Forest Rangers.

> *(Relieved the FOREST RANGERS move up stage and remove hats, gloves and packs)*

BILLY

Sure glad to hear that. Tell me, Chief, don't you Kadotas have a reservation?

CHIEF BROWN BEAR

Kadota Indians no live on reservation.

> *(Spreads arms to take in entire scene)*

All this belong to Kadotas. All!

BILLY

Does the United States know about that?

CHIEF BROWN BEAR

Fight many years to keep. Only two Kadotas left. Rest die fighting white man. Many white man die, too.

BILLY

> *(Raising arm)*

How!

CHIEF BROWN BEAR

How! In D.C. Washington, settle case by law. Better to fight with tomahawk than law suit but Merry Sunshine convince me to do this.

BILLY

Smart girl, Miss Mary.

CHIEF BROWN BEAR

Me visit her here each summer. She my adopted daughter. Me give her Indian name, Merry Sunshine. She merry like sunshine so me call her Merry Sunshine.

BILLY

That's very clever of you, Chief. Very clever. Now if you'll excuse me, I think I'd better go and *find* Miss Mary.

> *(Starts toward Inn)*

CHIEF BROWN BEAR

Stay! Here come Merry Sunshine *now.*

BILLY

> *(Turns sharply, raises arm)*

HOW!

CHIEF BROWN BEAR

No, *now!*

> *(Music in. As the FOREST RANGERS sing "LITTLE MARY SUN-SHINE," CHIEF BROWN BEAR retires U.R.)*

LITTLE MARY SUNSHINE

FOREST RANGERS
Refrain
> You've got to hand it to Little Mary Sunshine:
> Little Mary is the sunshine of the sun,
> You've got to hand it to Little Mary Sunshine:
> Little Mary has a smile for every one;
> She may be a bit old-fashioned, but then
> When you unlock your heart, sublime
> You've got to hand it to Little Mary Sunshine
> For she's very merry all the time.

(LITTLE MARY SUNSHINE (MARY POTTS) (Leading Lady-Soprano) makes a grand entrance from U.R. She is dressed in fashionable gardening clothes of the period. She clutches a large bouquet of flowers. She pauses at tree U.R., hands flowers to BILLY and greeting the FOREST RANGERS SHE moves D.C. for the song's Interlude)

(BILLY deposits flowers OFF-RIGHT and joins the RANGERS)

LITTLE MARY	It's nice to see you all again
RANGERS	It's nice to be here, Little Mary
LITTLE MARY	It's nice to have you call again
RANGERS	It's nice to see dear Little Mary
LITTLE MARY	But when you go away again I want to say again Oh, thanks so much For all you've done for Little Mary Sunshine But don't forget to keep in touch
LITTLE MARY	It's nice to have you here again
RANGERS	It's such a pleasure, Little Mary
LITTLE MARY	It's nice to have you near again
RANGERS	You're such a treasure, Little Mary
LITTLE MARY	But when it's time to go again You've got to know again I'll never pine Your love and care will stay with Little Mary But don't forget to drop a line

(As the FOREST RANGERS repeat the refrain, LITTLE MARY chimes in with a "ha-ha-ha" Soprano obligato)

2nd Refrain

LITTLE MARY
& RANGERS
	You've got to hand it to Little Mary Sunshine:
	   Little Mary is the sunshine of the sun;
	You've got to hand it to Little Mary Sunshine:
	   Little Mary has a smile for every one;
	She may be a bit old-fashioned, but then
	   When you unlock your heart, sublime
	You've got to hand it to Little Mary Sunshine
	   For she's very merry all the time.

(Dialogue after song)

LITTLE MARY

Welcome; welcome all of you to my humble Inn, 'though if I had known you were coming, I should have arranged some pleasant evening's festivities for you: a lecture, perhaps, by the local minister or an amateur String Quartet.

(Xing R.)

As it is, all that I've planned is a small garden party for some ladies who arrived this very day from the East and I'm sure a party with them would hold no interest for you.

BILLY

Ladies? Old ladies or young ladies?

LITTLE MARY

(Xing L. to C.)

Oh, young ladies. I should say none is scarce past twenty and one, whatever difference that might make. I'm truly sorry I even mentioned it.

BILLY

(Xing to Mary)

On the contrary, a bevy of young ladies is a welcome contrast to a Forest Ranger's usual diet of flora and fauna. We accept your hospitality and kindness and only wish we could in some way help you in your present difficulty.

LITTLE MARY

My present difficulty, dear Corporal?

BILLY

Is it not true, Miss Mary, that you built this charming Inn on a site you purchased from the United States Government, with the meager savings you earned through selling your home-made cookies?

LITTLE MARY

That is true, dear Corporal.

BILLY

And is it not true that because you have been unable to meet the payments on the land the Government will be forced to foreclose their mortgage?

LITTLE MARY

Indeed, that is quite true; but to what present difficulty do you refer?

BILLY

Why, the mortgage, Miss Mary. If the mortgage is foreclosed you will be cast out and penniless.

LITTLE MARY

In truth, I'm surprised that you would think that such a little thing as this would disturb me.

(Xing L.)

I am but sorely grieved that it disturbs you. Listen:

(Music in: LOOK FOR A SKY OF BLUE)

LOOK FOR A SKY OF BLUE

(LITTLE MARY and FOREST RANGERS)

LITTLE MARY

Verse

Don't be sad and gloomy
Come and harken to me
    Please be gay
There's no time for tear drops
When there's rain we hear drops
    But they quickly fade away
Just because we haven't got a penny in our pockets
And life seems a great morass;
    Pray, don't be offended,
    Kind thoughts are intended:
You don't see the cheery side; alas:

	LITTLE MARY (con't.)
1st Refrain	When e'er a cloud appears
	Filled with doubt and fears
	Look for a sky of blue
	When e'er a cloud of grey
	Seems to waft your way
	Look for a sky of blue
	Remember, sometimes the sun is shining
	It may be shining some day for you-oo-oo-oo-oo
	So 'til that happy day
	We must learn to say
	"Look for a sky of blue"
2nd Refrain	When e'er a cloud appears
	Filled with doubt and fears
	Look for a sky of blue
FOREST RANGERS	A sky of blue
LITTLE MARY	When e'er a cloud of grey
	Seems to waft your way
	Look for a sky of blue
FOREST RANGERS	A sky of blue
LITTLE MARY	Remember, sometimes
FOREST RANGERS	Sometimes
LITTLE MARY	The sun is shining
FOREST RANGERS	Shining
LITTLE MARY	It may be shining
FOREST RANGERS	Shining
MARY & RANGERS	Some day for you-oo-oo-oo-oo

(*Little MARY dances with FOREST RANGERS*)

MARY & RANGERS	So 'til that happy day
	We must learn to say
FOREST RANGERS	We're saying
MARY & RANGERS	Look for a sky of . . .
LITTLE MARY	Blue
FOREST RANGERS	A sky of blue.

(*After the song, CAPTAIN JIM enters from the Inn, crosses to Little Mary and salutes her*)

CAPTAIN JIM

Captain Big Jim Warington at your service, Miss Mary.

LITTLE MARY

Welcome, Captain Jim.
(*Xing L.*)
How sorry I am that I wasn't here to greet you on your arrival but I was in the garden saying "hello" to my flowers.

CAPTAIN JIM

Think nought of it, Miss Mary. Your maid has arranged everything for the billeting of my men.

LITTLE MARY
Dear Nancy. I should be lost without dear, dear Nancy.

CAPTAIN JIM
Corporal.

BILLY
(Saluting and Xing to Captain Jim)
Yes, Sir?

CAPTAIN JIM
Take the men to their quarters, Corporal. I assume you know Miss Mary's maid, Nancy?

BILLY
Yes, Sir. Only too well, Sir. We used to be, . . . very close, Sir.

CAPTAIN JIM
You will find her invaluable in taking care of the men's needs.

BILLY
Yes, Sir. That's what I'm afraid of, Sir.

CAPTAIN JIM
Dismissed, Corporal.

BILLY
(Saluting)
Yes, Sir.
(To Forest Rangers)
Troop, 'tention! Left face! Double time, march!
(The FOREST RANGERS exit U.L. of Inn, Billy almost clears stage then remembers The Book of Rules & Regulations which he has left on tree stump during the preceding scene. He quickly crosses to stump, picks up book and says:)
Rules and Regulations. Yes, Sir. Thank you, Sir.
(Exits U.L.)

CAPTAIN JIM
It is indeed kind of you, Miss Mary, to once again make your Inn available to my men and myself.

LITTLE MARY
So long as the Colorado Inn remains mine, dear Corporal, I hope you will look on it as a respite from your dangerous adventures, however brief and fleeting those occasions must necessarily be.

CAPTAIN JIM
Brief and fleeting they are, Miss Mary, yet dare I say that these infrequent meetings are the oasises in the vast desert of a poor Forest Ranger's lonely life.

LITTLE MARY
I am but pleased, dear Captain, to learn that two hearts meet in this relationship: for indeed, we are two dearest and truest of friends.

CAPTAIN JIM
(Backs away one step from Little Mary)
Friends, Miss Mary?

LITTLE MARY
(One step to Captain Jim)
The very best, dear Captain.

CAPTAIN JIM

(One step to Little Mary)
Would that I were able to pursue the subject further,
(Xing R.)
but when a man's life is in danger . . .

LITTLE MARY

In danger? Oh, Captain Jim, would it be presumptuous of me to inquire in what danger your life might be?

CAPTAIN JIM

I'll tell you, Miss Mary: from Canada to the Mexican Border a notorious band of Indians has ravished the land of wild game and wantonly set the forests afire. Until now they have evaded the hand of justice but their hiding place has been discovered, not far from here, and it is my assignment to take their leader, dead or alive.

LITTLE MARY

(Xing to Captain Jim)
Oh, Captain Jim, I'm frightened for you.

CAPTAIN JIM

Do not fret, Miss Mary, for if the Indian guide who will lead me there can be trusted, I have no fears. Tell me, Miss Mary, by chance do you happen to know anything about a tribe of Indians called the Kadotas?

LITTLE MARY

The Kadotas! Indeed I do, for when I was but a tiny tot, I lost my way while berry picking and was found by the then savage Kadota Indians. I was taken to Chief Brown Bear, their leader and he brought me up as his adopted daughter. Chief Brown Bear is the only father I've ever known.

CAPTAIN JIM

I see. Then you might know my guide. He goes by the name of Fleet Foot.

LITTLE MARY

Fleet Foot! Why he's the very Indian brave who found me in the forest and saved my life. A finer guide you couldn't find and as for being trusted, why, I'd stake my life on it. Oh, I'm so relieved, Captain Jim. Fleet Foot is my Indian Father's closest friend. Their bond is very deep . . . They're the only two Kadotas left.

CAPTAIN JIM

(Quizzically)
The only two?

LITTLE MARY

The only two.
(Xing U.L.)
Oh, how happy Indian Father will be to learn that Fleet Foot is here.

CAPTAIN JIM

For the present, Miss Mary, I would prefer to keep Fleet Foot's arrival a deep secret.

LITTLE MARY

(Coming D.C. to Captain Jim)
Oh, then my knowledge is a sealed book, dear Captain.

CAPTAIN JIM

And now, Miss Mary, with Fleet Foot's arrival imminent, would it be audacious of me to ask for your dear companionship?

LITTLE MARY
Audacious, Captain? Why that's the very least a woman can do.
      (*Xing D.C.*)
Would you care to stroll in my garden? So many flowers have blossomed
and bloomed since last you were here you shall scarce recognize it.

CAPTAIN JIM
Well, I know and love your garden, Miss Mary, yet before we saunter hand
in hand into that feast of loveliness my honest nature wrings a confession
from me.

LITTLE MARY
A confession, Captain Jim?

CAPTAIN JIM
A confession, Miss Mary:
      (*Music in, YOU'RE THE FAIREST FLOWER, as CAPTAIN JIM
      walks LITTLE MARY downstage*)

Act I

SCENE 2

*The Garden. The Garden drop comes down in front of
the Colorado Inn setting. CAPTAIN JIM sings to LITTLE
MARY.*
      YOU'RE THE FAIREST FLOWER

CAPTAIN JIM

Verse

'Though I love your garden
      With its pretty posies
You must beg its pardon
      If my heart discloses
What is but its duty
      In its honest way
To declare a beauty
      Lovelier, far, than they:
Ah, . . .

Refrain

You're the fairest flower
In this bower, dear,
      You're the frailest blossom
      Gossamer
'Though you're such a shy Miss
      Shy Miss, I disclose:
You're the fairest flower on earth,
      An American Beauty Rose.

Interlude

Iris and hollyhocks
      I can see them still;
Pink pinks and frilly phlox,
      Dainty daffodil,
Sweet pea and marigold
      I can see them there,
Poppies of fairy gold
      Modest maiden hair,

CAPTAIN JIM (con't.)
The teasing tulips gently wave
　　At every passing breeze
The pampered pansies slyly crave
　　To bring us to our knees
Flowers tall
　　Flowers small
　　　　I love them all
And yet, they do but imitate
The fairest one of all:

Refrain　　　For you're the fairest flower
In this bower, dear,
　　You're the frailest blossom
　　Gossamer
'Though you're such a shy Miss
　　Shy Miss. I disclose:
You're the fairest flower on earth
　　An American Beauty Rose.

(At the end of the song the voice of MME. ERNESTINE VON LIEBEDICH can be heard off-stage. She sings the first line of ACH, DU LIEBER AUGUSTIN, unaccompanied. LITTLE MARY rises and puts her hand to her ear)

LITTLE MARY

Listen, dear Captain.

CAPTAIN JIM

It sound like someone singing.
(We hear ERNESTINE'S "echo" sing the line back)

LITTLE MARY

It is someone singing and I'd recognize that glorious voice anywhere. It's Madame Ernestine Von Liebedich.
(ERNESTINE takes in the mountain air as she makes her entrance from D.L. She is past middle age; plump and friendly. She has a strong German accent and a booming contralto voice. She is dressed in heavy tweeds and carries a leafy twig)

ERNESTINE

(Turning, she sees Little Mary)
Ah, mine liebchen, mine puppchen. You miss der hike mit me today, ya?

LITTLE MARY

Do forgive me, Madame, but a dear friend arrived unexpectedly.

ERNESTINE

Hear you der echo of der singing?

LITTLE MARY

Oh, very clearly, Madame.

ERNESTINE

Der echo iss alvays der same, it matter not vere. It take me back to der kinderhood. Ya, ya; how often as der kinder I make der echo.

LITTLE MARY

Madame, I would like you to meet a dear, dear friend of mine: Captain Warington.

CAPTAIN JIM

(Salutes her)
Captain "Big Jim" Warington at your service, Madame.

— 11 —

ERNESTINE

(Xing R. to Captain Jim)

Dis der unexpected friend, ya? Iss pleasure to meet you, Captain. Mine liebchen speak of no von else all der day long, so I say to her, "Liebchen, iss time you get dis Captain to tink of der marriage."

LITTLE MARY

(Embarrassed)

Madame Ernestine is our most celebrated guest. We consider it a great honor that an opera singer of her stature chooses to spend her leisure with us.

ERNESTINE

Is much like der homeland here, Captain. And we all long for der home, ya? Tell me, Captain, ven you settle down with vife und home?

LITTLE MARY

But, Madame Ernestine, Captain Warington leads a very active life. You see, as a Forest Ranger, he can't be in any one place for very long.

ERNESTINE

Das is bad, Captain. Der life of der Zigeuner, der gypsy iss not for you, I tink. You need der home, der wife, der kinder. Und right now you need der hike. You look tired, Captain, very tired. A nice long hike mit der liebchen to talk over dez tings: dat make you feel much better.

LITTLE MARY

But, Madame Ernestine, Captain Warington has just marched from the Mexican Border.

ERNESTINE

Ya; dat good valk. You keep dat up, Captain, und you get over dat tired feeling. But der hike; der hike is for der boy und der girl. I remember in der homeland ve have der hiking club; und alvays der boy und der girl togeder. Rocky Mountains not so different from Bavarian Alps. Togeder you see der snow-capped mountains, der gentle valley und far, far below der vinding rifer. Iss make two very close. Und breeze. Tell me, Captain, do you breeze?

CAPTAIN JIM

I beg your pardon, Madame?

ERNESTINE

Breeze.

(Breathes)

Breeze deep.

(Breathes deeply)

Fill up der diaphragm; like der singer. Der mountain air put new life in body. It makes der man der man und der voman der voman. Let us all breeze!

(The THREE breathe deeply)

Enough. Iss like giving der rich cream to von who has only had der skim milk. But now you iss ready for der hike, ya?

LITTLE MARY

Captain Warington will be here only a short while, Madame Ernestine, and I'm afraid he'll just have time to see the garden.

ERNESTINE

Iss pity. Der stroll in der garden iss not so good as der hike in der mountains but den, ven you vant to, you Americans can vork with quickness, ya, Captain?

(Shaking his hand)

Much good luck to you, Captain.

— 12 —

LITTLE MARY

Oh, please do join us, Madame.

ERNESTINE

No, no, mine liebchen. Der stroll iss for der two. Now go; go; go.

CAPTAIN JIM

It was an honor to meet you, Madame. I hope I have the pleasure of hearing you sing one day.

ERNESTINE

I tink, maybe, I not sing so much now, Captain.

CAPTAIN JIM

I would be sorry to hear that.

ERNESTINE

Veil, maybe vun day I sing for both of you: Der Brahms' Lullaby!
(Embarrassed beyond belief LITTLE MARY exits L.)
Auf wiedersehen.

CAPTAIN JIM

(Salutes her)
Madame.
(CAPTAIN JIM exits L.)

ERNESTINE

Iss good: iss right und iss alvays der same. It matter not vere. Der Homeland under der yout, dey iss gone for me.
(Music in under dialogue)
Yet dey iss nefer really gone, for dey vill alvays be here, in mine heart.
(ERNESTINE sings:)
IN IZZENSCHNOOKEN ON THE LOVELY ESSENZOOK ZEE

ERNESTINE

Refrain   In Izzenschnooken on da luffly Essenzook Zee
I often seem to often dream how happy I'd be
    Da Dasserschtunken Mountains
        All vitened mit schnow
    Da Vasserfunken River
        Far below
    I close mine eyes und see dem all;
        Da peace und da joy
    Ven I vas but a puppchen girl
        Mit my liebster boy
Vile hand in hand ve vondered und vandered so free
In Izzenschnooken on da luffly Essenzook Zee.
(Music continues under the following spoken dialogue)
Ya; I remember dem vell; — dos happy days, — dos carefree places; so far avay und so very long ago, — But I do not forget da land of mine kinder for dat, — dat vas, — Home.
(She sings)
    I close mine eyes und see dem all:
        Da peace und da joy
    Ven I vas but a puppchen girl
        Mit my liebster boy
Vile hand in hand ve vondered und vandered so free
In Izzenschnooken on da luffly Essenzook Zee.
(ERNESTINE "blows a kiss" at

BLACKOUT!

Act I

*The Inn. Discovered are CORA, MAUD, GWENDOLYN,
BLANCH, HENRIETTA and MABEL. They are young
ladies from Eastchester Finishing School (LADIES OF
THE ENSEMBLE). Ad libs and girlish squeals can be
heard over the gay music as we watch them playing
croquet. In a few moments they sing:*
    PLAYING CROQUET

YOUNG LADIES

1st Refrain

Playing croquet

Is a wonderful way
To enjoy an afternoon
Hitting the ball through the wicket
Pushing the ball isn't cricket
What can be done
That is barrels of fun
Yet refined and most polite
Play croquet is a wonderful way
If there's not a man in sight
And there's not a man in sight.
(Stamping mallets)

Interlude

Young Ladies from Eastchester Finishing School
Are ever so very well bred
Young Ladies from Eastchester Finishing School
Not well bred would rather be dead
Of French and Greek we've a passing command
Pianofortes we're playing
Most words we use are so terribly grand
We can't understand what we're saying
When we shan't do this and we shan't do that
We bring forth a haughty stare

When we can't play this and we can't play that
We've mastered some poses
We do with our noses
While sticking them up in the air
But this game has been passed by the Dean
If we're ever so careful our limbs are not seen
And so . . .

2nd Refrain

Playing croquet
Is a wonderful way
To enjoy an afternoon
Striking the ball with the mallet
Yours won't hit my ball, — or shall it?
Tossing one's curls
Isn't proper for girls
Who is breeding do abound
But playing croquet
Is a wonderful way
If there's not a man around
And there's not a man around!
*(After the song the YOUNG LADIES relax from
their game)*

MAUD

Oh, isn't it exciting to be in the wild Rocky Mountains of Colorado!

HENRIETTA

Oh, yes! And there's nothing like a game of croquet to make a girl feel reckless.

GWENDOLYN

It's a pity there aren't any eligible young bachelors to see us at our headstrong best. For we *are* pretty.

MAUD

We *are* socially prominent.

HENRIETTA

And *ever* so rich.

CORA

We can thank our lucky stars the game of croquet has been approved.

BLANCH

I should say. What ever would a girl do all day?

GWENDOLYN

One can re-read Jane Austen just so many times.

MAUD

And, oh, what fun this evening shall be. Imagine a garden party.

HENRIETTA

It's a pity we'll be the only ones there.

CORA

But you must admit, dear, it will be properly exclusive.

GWENDOLYN

Let's on to the game.

HENRIETTA

I'm tired of playing croquet. I want to do something that *hasn't* been approved: something *daring*.

CORA

Something daring?

HENRIETTA

Yes, something daring; like, like swinging on that swing over there.
(HENRIETTA crosses to swing hanging R.)

BLANCH

Swinging on a swing!

CORA

Good heavens, Henrietta, what will *they* say?

HENRIETTA

They aren't here. *No* one's here at all, so I can't see the harm. Look. Mabel's found a swing, too.
(MABEL at the swing L., smiles)

MAUD

I think it's quite outrageous.

CORA

Oh, Maud, so do I, dear.

GWENDOLYN

I'm not sure we should look.

HENRIETTA

Then no one shall see us in the whole wide world and we can swing to our heart's content.

(Music in, SWINGING)

(HENRIETTA and MABEL climb into the swings. They are pushed by the other young ladies)

SWINGING

(Young Ladies)

YOUNG LADIES

Refrain

> Swinging, swinging
> Up in the air we are winging
> Flying, flying it's much too high
> Trying, trying to touch the sky
> While we're swinging, swinging
> Letting our fancies take flight
> But a Young Lady learns
> That she's got to take turns
> If there's not a man in sight
> *(Looking out)*

And there's not a man in, —

> *(The YOUNG LADIES stop all action as BUSTER, A FOREST RANGER, enters to music and salutes Gwendolyn)*

GWENDOLYN

(Spoken) A man!

> *(SLIM, another FOREST RANGER, enters and salutes Henrietta)*

HENRIETTA

(Spoken) Another man!

> *(The remaining FOREST RANGERS enter and approach the remaining YOUNG LADIES)*

YOUNG LADIES

(Sung) And there's now a man in sight!

> *(The FOREST RANGERS sing the following in two part harmony as the YOUNG LADIES listen in rapt attention)*
> HOW DO YOU DO
> (Tenors and Baritones)

FOREST RANGERS

> How do you do: how do you do;
> That's very proper a "How do you do"
> What a fine day: what a fine day;
> That's very proper a "What a fine day"
> Haven't you heard, haven't you heard
> It's so very proper to say a kind word
> Is there a way that will lead you to say
> A "How do you do" today
> *(Obviously deciding they will have none of it the YOUNG LADIES return to their games; completely ignoring the RANGERS. A refrain is sung in three part counterpoint:)*

HOW DO YOU DO (Ten. & Bar.)	*PLAYING CROQUET* (Sopranos)	*SWINGING* (Altos)
How do you do	Playing croquet	Swinging, swinging
How do you do	Is a wonderful way	Up in the air
That's very proper	To enjoy an	We are winging
A "How do you do"	Afternoon	
Etc.	Etc.	Etc.

(SOPRANOS and ALTOS together)
And there's not a man in sight

ALL

How do you do	No, there's not	No, there's not
Today?	A man in sight	A man in sight

CORA

I am sorry, sir, to tell you that you will be unable to engage us in conversation.

PETE

But most certainly you can return a simple, "How do you do?"

CORA

I'm afraid not. Perhaps a "Thank you", a "Thank you" is quite past indefinite; but a "How do you do", a "How do you do" does border on the indelicate personal. Your attempt has been a noble one and we want to thank you, . . .

YOUNG LADIES

(Curtseying)
Thank you.

CORA

But when a young lady of breeding has been brought up with a standard of, . . . Blanch! Are you allowing that young man to whisper in your ear?

BLANCH

I'm afraid so, Cora.

CORA

Have we forgotten who we are?

YOUNG LADIES

(Curtseying)
Young Ladies from Eastchester Finishing School.

HENRIETTA

But couldn't we forget it; for just this once!

GWENDOLYN

For we *are* pretty.

MAUD

We *are* socially prominent.

HENRIETTA

And *ever* so rich!

CORA

I am more than willing to concede that it would not be difficult to form an attachment for one of these young men; but we must be strong; all of us, for it is the weak link that breaks the chain; and so that none of us may slip I suggest that we immediately form a pact.

(By this time only THREE COUPLES remain)

HENRIETTA

But, Cora, I'm afraid our pact would have to be in the form of a trio.

GWENDOLYN

And that scarcely seems fair, now does it?

PETE, TEX & SLIM

(Bowing low)
How do you do?

CORA, HENRIETTA & GWENDOLYN

(Curtseying and smiling sweetly)
How do you do?

PETE

Would you be good enough to allow us to engage you in conversation?

CORA

And what is the nature of the conversation in which you wished to engage us?

PETE

We hoped you might be able to settle an argument we've been having amongst ourselves. It seems we can't decide if you are as beautiful and lovely as you seem, or if you are, on the whole, rather plain.

CORA, HENRIETTA & GWENDOLYN

Rather plain?

PETE, TEX & SLIM

Yes, rather plain.

CORA, HENRIETTA & GWENDOLYN

Oh!

PETE

You see, we've been away from feminine companionship for such a long while we feel that in judging a young lady's feminine pulchritude we might be, at least for the moment, overly indulgent.

SLIM

And Forest Rangers being the good looking dogs that they are, must necessarily associate with young ladies of comparable appearance.

TEX

It's one of the Forest Ranger's unwritten laws.

CORA

Would you mind repeating that question just-once-more?

Act I

SCENE 4

Primrose Path Traveler closes behind them.
(Music in, TELL A HANDSOME STRANGER-SEXTETTE, sung by
PETE and CORA, TEX and GWENDOLYN and SLIM and
HENRIETTA)
TELL A HANDSOME STRANGER
SEXTET
(PETE & CORA, SLIM & HENRIETTA, TEX & MABEL)

Introduction

GENTLEMEN	Tell a handsome stranger Are you pretty or a homely maid?
YOUNG LADIES	Modesty forbids me, Sir, To repeat what all concur
GENTLEMEN	Then tell a handsome stranger, If you're pretty, would you be afraid To take a little stroll with me? A kiss is what the toll would be
YOUNG LADIES	Dear me! Kind Sir, I'm such an honest Miss So honest that you should not ask me this
GENTLEMEN	But I do, —
YOUNG LADIES	Then I'll go
GENTLEMEN	And you're pretty too?
YOUNG LADIES	Now you know That it's so
ALL	I am (You are) pretty So we'll go: We'll go . . .

Refrain

GENTLEMEN	I'll take you down the Garden Path
YOUNG LADIES	Do!
GENTLEMEN	We'll watch the birdies have a bath
YOUNG LADIES	Oo!
GENTLEMEN	Beneath a tree we'll kiss
YOUNG LADIES	Oh, bliss!
GENTLEMEN	We'll be a loving girl and boy
YOUNG LADIES	Oh, joy! You make it sound so pretty that You make my little heart go pitty-pat
ALL	Oh, heavens above, I'm falling in love with you I fondly give my heart away It's yours forever and a day 'Twill last eternally Now that I love you and you love me.

(Doing a simple dance step, THEY stroll off arm in arm DR at the end of the number)

(After the Sexttette exits D.R., three FOREST RANGERS; HANK, BUSTER and TOM, enter, backing themselves in from D.L. HANK has an old fashioned camera on a tripod, and TOM a bird on a stick)

There. That's it, Miss Nancy. Don't move a muscle. Watch the birdie.
Ready: one, two, three.
*(Trying to be the "woman of the world", NANCY TWINKLE, our
soubrette, enters from D.L., still holding the pose of putting one
arm behind her head. She is dressed in a maid's outfit of the period)*

NANCY
Did you get the picture, fellows?

HANK
Sure did, Miss Nancy.

BUSTER
And it was a honey, eh, Hank?

HANK
Let's take one over here, in front of the flowers.
*(BUSTER gets bench from off-Right and places it stage R. for Nancy
to pose on)*

NANCY
Well, all right; but just one more.
(She sits and lifts skirt almost to knees)
How's this?

BUSTER
Wow! Let me take this one.
(Rushes behind camera)

HANK
(XING to R. of bench)
Would you think ill of me, Miss Nancy, if I were to pose with you? I'd like
to send a picture to my mother.

NANCY
Why, what a dear, sweet thought; you sit right down here.

HANK
(Joining her on bench)
And would you think ill of me, Miss Nancy, if I were to kiss you?

NANCY
To send to your mother?

HANK
Well, Mom always likes to see me happy.
(He holds her hands and kisses her cheek)

BUSTER
Hold it; that's it. Ready; one, two, three.
*(BILLY enters D.R. and an embarrassed NANCY TWINKLE rises
and crosses to him)*

NANCY
Oh, hello, Billy. I've been looking everywhere for you.

BILLY

So I see. Privates 'Tention!
(Crosses center and checks camera)
The next time you take pictures of a young lady I suggest you try putting film in the camera.
(Takes out Book of Rules and Regulations)
Your dishonesty in this matter could be a very serious offense, however, this time I intend to let you go. Privates, dismissed!
(HANK, BUSTER and TOM hurry out D.L., taking camera and equipment with them)

NANCY

Oh, Billy, how masterful you were. Just for that I'm going to give you a big welcome home kiss.

BILLY

Don't come any closer.
(Overly dramatic)
You may as well know right now: we're through, finished, washed up.

NANCY

But Billy, that's the way we were the last time you left. I want to change it all back again.

BILLY

I see; and I am but a puppet on a string dancing to your tune, as it were. Well, it won't do, Nancy. It won't do at all.

NANCY

Oh, Billy, I promise I won't so much as look at another man, ever again.

BILLY

If you but knew how much I want to trust you. Do you, do you really mean that?

NANCY

Of course I do, Billy.

BILLY

I don't believe you!
(Music in, ONCE IN A BLUE MOON, sung by BILLY and NANCY)
ONCE IN A BLUE MOON
(BILLY AND NANCY)

Introduction

BILLY   *(Angrily)*
I don't want to hear your promise
For I'm now a Doubting Thomas
Your behavior is an absolute disgrace;

NANCY   Oh, Billy

BILLY   If you swore upon a Bible
Then the church should sue for libel
And I'm not so sure they wouldn't win the case;

NANCY   That's silly

BILLY   For I've seen you kissing others
And you tell me they're your brothers
Do you grow them by the bushel or the bale?

NANCY	Who, me?
BILLY	Or you tell me they're your cousins, You've got cousins by the dozens, And it's mighty strange that every one's a male:
NANCY	Well, you see, — — —
BILLY	If I'm slower than molasses It's these rosy colored glasses But from now on all my faith and trust is gone.
NANCY	Oh, no!
BILLY	For I've reached a big decision What I need is better vision: You're not worth the paper that you're written on!
NANCY	Oh!?
BILLY	You've made your bed a rolling stone And now the shoe won't fit You've had your cake and should have known You'd have to lay in it! *(Softening with remembrance)* Yet, — — —

Refrain

BILLY	Once in a blue moon I think you love me
NANCY	I often think I'd like to love you
BILLY	Once in a blue moon I think you don't
NANCY	It's rather pleasing To be so teasing
BILLY	Once in a blue moon I think you hate me
NANCY	I only hate you 'cause I love you
BILLY	Once in a blue moon I think you won't
NANCY	I'm undecided And must be guided
BILLY	Once in a blue moon you want to leave me
NANCY	I can't imagine why I'd leave you
BILLY	Once in a blue moon you're in a whirl
NANCY	You set me reeling With such a feeling
TOGETHER	Why this confusion? Here's the conclusion: I am your once in a blue moon girl. You are my

Act I

SCENE 5

The Primrose Path, a scrim, opens to The Inn as BILLY and NANCY move upstage to do a SOFT-SHOE DANCE. THEY exit singing.

TOGETHER Why this confusion?
Here's the conclusion:
I am your
        once in a blue moon girl . . . a blue moon girl
You are my
(NANCY and BILLY exit R)
(LITTLE MARY and CAPTAIN JIM enter U.R.
LITTLE MARY crosses to the Inn porch)

LITTLE MARY

There now, I do believe I've shown you everything but the amaryllis.
   (XING D.R.)
Ah, the amaryllis, dear Captain; the amaryllis are dearer than ever.
   (Sitting on bench)
But for shame, dear Captain, for I do perceive that your mind does wander.

CAPTAIN JIM

Truly, Miss Mary, you do perceive me incorrectly, for never could my mind wander from such a one as you. On the contrary, with every fiber of my being I do try to control myself from saying the words that cannot yet be spoken.

LITTLE MARY

Words that cannot be spoken? I do confess I burn with a young maiden's innocent curiosity.

CAPTAIN JIM

   (XING behind bench)
Press me not further, Miss Mary. Soon enough you shall hear them should I return safely from my mission.

LITTLE MARY

With Fleet Foot at your side I have no fear for your safe return and so, you see, dear Captain, you do leave me in cruel suspense for nought.

CAPTAIN JIM

'Tis a most tempting time and place; and we are quite alone.
   (He sits beside her)

LITTLE MARY

Alone, dear Captain?
   (Rising and crossing L.)
No, not quite, Look; in yonder tree, my dear little Coo-coo bird sits peeping at us.
   (LITTLE MARY calls "coo-coo" twice to her bird)

CAPTAIN JIM

   (Xing to Little Mary)
Yes, but aside from the Coo-coo bird we are quite alone.

LITTLE MARY

   (Xing to Little Mary)
Yes, yes, we are quite alone.

CAPTAIN JIM
(Xing R. to above Little Mary he turns L. to face her)
Now; now I may ask you the question,
(Takes her hand)
the question that has been burning in my heart for, lo, these many months.

LITTLE MARY
(Takes her hand away, puts it to her mouth and calls off R.)
Yoo hoo. Nancy. Oh, Nancy.
(To Captain Jim)
Excuse me, dear Captain; I must have Nancy prepare you some refreshments for your journey.

CAPTAIN JIM
But Miss Mary . . . .

LITTLE MARY
Now, we can't have you going hungry this evening, can we? I shan't be a moment.
(She exits R.)
(In pantomime CAPTAIN JIM practices how he will pour forth his heart. As he tries the bended knee approach BILLY enters R., kneels and salutes)

CAPTAIN JIM
(Rising)
Oh, Corporal; I, I thought you were someone else.

BILLY
(Rising)
Yes, Sir. Miss Mary asked me to tell you that she shall return momentarily.

CAPTAIN JIM
Thank you, Corporal. That should give us time for the brief chat I want to have with you.

BILLY
Yes, Sir?

CAPTAIN JIM
Corporal, in a short while a trusted guide will be here to lead me to the notorious Indian band for whom we have searched so long. During my absence I want you to take command of the troop.

BILLY
Oh, yes, Sir.

CAPTAIN JIM
Until nine o'clock this evening.

BILLY
Until nine o'clock, Sir?

CAPTAIN JIM
It is my mission to bring in their leader, dead or alive. As a Forest Ranger I hope to appeal to his sense of honor, for his accomplices will be disbanded and freed, but if I have not returned by nine o'clock, it will then become *your* duty to apprehend this killer by more devious means.

BILLY
M-my duty, Sir?

CAPTAIN JIM

The guide will return to take you to his hideout. There, disguised as an Indian Brave, you will join their campfire unnoticed. You will wait for the proper moment to strike, then, BANG! single-handed you will hold the others at bay as you take their leader to justice. You'll be a hero, Corporal, ...

BILLY

Me, Sir?

CAPTAIN JIM

If it works.

BILLY

Are you sure some of the other fellows don't want to come along? I don't want to hog all the glory.

CAPTAIN JIM

It's a one man job, Corporal. Should I not return you have my personal good wishes for your success, but should you fail, you too will have the pleasure of knowing that you have not died in vain. We will have died for a noble cause.

BILLY

I feel better already.

CAPTAIN JIM

Ah, but I see dear Little Mary approaching. You're dismissed, Corporal Jester.

BILLY

Yes, Sir.
        (Billy wanders off L. above the Inn)
        (CAPTAIN JIM crosses R. and meets LITTLE MARY, who is aiding a very elderly INDIAN to hobble in)

LITTLE MARY

Look dear Captain; look who I spied.

CAPTAIN JIM

Poor old fellow. There you go.
        (Helps him to bench)
I wonder who he is?

LITTLE MARY

        (Surprised)
Why, this is my dear friend, Fleet Foot.

CAPTAIN JIM

This is Fleet Foot?

LITTLE MARY

The finest guide in the West. Now, don't you worry about Fleet Foot. He'd know this territory blindfolded.
        (FLEET FOOT dozes off. LITTLE MARY nudges him and he speaks)

FLEET FOOT

Um ton go la, Merry Sunshine. Um ton go la. Shaun ta goo ka? Shaun ta goo ka, Brown Bear?

LITTLE MARY

Cha ka, Brown Bear. Soo taun cha. Soo taun cha Brown Bear dun ·ka la fel. Fel sha ta Captain. Moe vay sha, Captain Warington.

FLEET FOOT
(Inspecting him closely)
Ah. Kadota doe hoot may. Doe hoot may saun cha. Saun cha.

LITTLE MARY
He says he's extremely honored to meet the man respected by Indians and whites alike.
(FLEET FOOT dozes off again)

CAPTAIN JIM
Tell him I am pleased that he has volunteered to act as my guide, but he need not risk his life in a matter that does not concern him; he can draw me a map instead.

LITTLE MARY
(Sits on bench next to FLEET FOOT and wakes him up)
Con say cha; da hoo. Fel taun cha, taun cha he.

FLEET FOOT
(Rising angrily)
Ka jo rah he! Da jo rah he may cha fay do ha!
(He goes into a coughing spell)

LITTLE MARY
(Rising and going to Fleet Foot)
He say, he must go with you. He must go with you and help capture this man who is a blot on the honor of all Indians. Shun a ton wah?
(Speaking closer to his ear)
Shun a ton wah . . . *WAH.*

FLEET FOOT
(Shaking his head sadly)
Gone wah ha, Merry Sunshine. Gone wah ha.
(He crosses L. and turns back to Little Mary)
Con day cha moo vay ha. Soon too cha. Wha ha she. Wah ha she.

LITTLE MARY
Wah ha she.
(FLEET FOOT walks straight into the porch. Recovering his dignity he wanders cautiously off U.R.)

FLEET FOOT
(Exiting)
Gone wah ha, Merry Sunshine. Gone wah ha.
(Waving "Good-bye," LITTLE MARY watches FLEET FOOT's exit intently for fear he will bump into something. After his exit she turns to Captain Jim)

LITTLE MARY
He'll be at the watering hole where he has two Indian ponies waiting. He wouldn't tell me the name of the Indian you were after. He said I should ask you.

CAPTAIN JIM
That seems strange. His name is Yellow Feather.

LITTLE MARY
(Clutching throat)
Yellow Feather!

CAPTAIN JIM
What is it, Miss Mary?

Yellow Feather!

CAPTAIN JIM

What is it? Do you know him?

LITTLE MARY

Yellow Feather is the son of Chief Brown Bear, but, but he's dead. We all thought him dead.

CAPTAIN JIM

I'm afraid he's very much alive.

LITTLE MARY

(XING L.)

I grew up with Yellow Feather. He heaped nothing but dishonor on his poor, dear father. Then, several years ago while on but another drunken orgy with a wanton woman, he knifed a man who accused him of cheating at cards. He was taken to jail, but, with his usual craftiness, he broke out and came here. You see, he is by tribal custom, a brother of mine, but I refused him help in his lawlessness. The sheriff and his men followed him here and he leaped over Point Look-Out, into the river below. Though his body was never found, we presumed him dead. I, I told Indian Father that he had died trying to save my life so that he could remember him with honor. Oh, Captain Jim, if Chief Brown Bear were to learn the truth, it would break his poor, old Indian heart.

CAPTAIN JIM

It is possible he need never know. Rest assured, Miss Mary, I shall do everything in my power to spare him this knowledge.

LITTLE MARY

(XING to him)

God bless you, Captain Jim. I deeply appreciate your concern for Chief Brown Bear.

CAPTAIN JIM

It would be dishonest of me were I not to say that my main concern in this matter is for *your* peace of mind, Miss Mary.

LITTLE MARY

My peace of mind, Captain Jim?

CAPTAIN JIM

(Taking her hand)

I have but a few moments before I must leave, Little Mary, ...

LITTLE MARY

Oh, dear, how thoughtless of me:
(Taking her hand away)
Your refreshments for your journey.
(XING to Inn stairs)
I'll fetch them at once.

CAPTAIN JIM

(XING to her)

Stay, Little Mary; I must be heard, for my refreshment, my feast, is but to have you near my side.

LITTLE MARY

Captain Jim!

CAPTAIN JIM

How many goodbyes we have said in the past, yet this time my heart can be still no longer: Little Mary, if I return, . . . will you be mine?

LITTLE MARY

Be yours? But, Captain, ...

CAPTAIN JIM

(On bended knee)

Oh, I know I am not worthy to ask for the hand of the dearest, the fairest, the loveliest flower that God ever gave to brighten this cold world of ours, but I ask, I ask for your hand all the same.

LITTLE MARY

Oh, Captain Jim, I had not allowed myself to hope, I would not allow myself to think; yet sometimes, sometimes in my wildest dreams, I secretly dared to pretend this happy moment would come about. Oh, rise, dear Captain, for my answer is yes; a thousand times, yes.

CAPTAIN JIM

(Rises and takes her hand)

Oh, Little Mary, . . .

LITTLE MARY

Yes!?

CAPTAIN JIM

If I return, . . .

LITTLE MARY

(Putting her fingers to his lips)

When you return, dear Captain.

CAPTAIN JIM

When I return; here we shall share our lives together and I shall be the happiest man alive.

LITTLE MARY

And, I, . . . a woman fulfilled.

(Music in, COLORADO LOVE CALL, sung by CAPTAIN JIM and LITTLE MARY)

COLORADO LOVE CALL
(CAPTAIN JIM & LITTLE MARY)

1st Refrain

CAPTAIN JIM &
LITTLE MARY

You-oo-oo and I
Shall live and die
Underneath a Colorado sky
Very soon
We'll have our June
Underneath a Colorado moon

CAPTAIN JIM

Each moment I'm away
My heart will pray
That soon I may
Return to where you'll be

LITTLE MARY

Each moment you are gone
My love lives on
From dawn to dawn
'Till you come back to me;
Come back to me

BOTH	Then
	    You-oo-oo and I
	  Shall live and die
	Underneath a Colorado sky
	  'Til then I'll try
	  To say goodbye:

Interlude

CAPTAIN JIM	My heart can only wait for you
LITTLE MARY	My heart is waiting for you too
BOTH	And with this promise to be true
CAPTAIN JIM	'Twill see me through
LITTLE MARY	'Twill see me through
CAPTAIN JIM	And yet I'll count the lonely hours
LITTLE MARY	I'll count the lonely hours
CAPTAIN JIM	'Til we can be as one
LITTLE MARY	'Til we can be as one
CAPTAIN JIM	As one
LITTLE MARY	As one

2nd Refrain

CAPTAIN JIM &
LITTLE MARY
	When
	    You-oo-oo and I
	  Shall live and die
	Underneath a Colorado sky
	    Very soon
	  We'll have our June
	Underneath a Colorado moon

CAPTAIN JIM	'Though I must leave
	  You must believe
	  My lonely heart will grieve
	    'Til then I must be stern

LITTLE MARY	And for your sake
	My lonely heart will ache
	And quake and break
	  If you do not return
	  My heart will yearn,
	  And burn
	  So please return

BOTH	Then
	  You-oo-oo and I
	  Shall live and die
	Underneath a Colorado sky
	  'Til then I'll try
	  To say goodbye:

LITTLE MARY	Goodbye, goodbye,
CAPTAIN JIM	Goodbye;

LITTLE MARY	Goodbye, goodbye,
CAPTAIN JIM	Goodbye;
BOTH	Goodbye!

(A dramatic musical coda follows as the TWO LOVERS separate and exit: LITTLE MARY L., CAPTAIN JIM, R.)

(The lights dim and CHIEF BROWN BEAR enters U.R. as if in a trance. He moves to C. and sits cross-legged. He raises his head to the sky and calls to the heavens:)

CHIEF BROWN BEAR

Ya too! Ho may ton go la! Ho may ton go la! Saun cha Beelee Jes-ter! Sa hay kee tow, Bee-lee Jester? Ra hoe may. Ra hoe may da koo cha. Shaun te Kadota!

(CHIEF BROWN BEAR remains motionless, arms crossed as BILLY enters from the Inn thumbing his Book of Rules and Regulations. BILLY moves D.L.)

BILLY

Oh, here it is:
(Reading)
"Desertion: desertion from the United States Forest Rangers is punishable by life imprisonment, death before a firing squad,
(Turning page)
or both." Or both?
(Turning to go, he sees Chief Brown Bear)
Oh, Chief; I didn't see you there. Did you fall down?
(BILLY tries to help Chief Brown Bear up but CHIEF BROWN BEAR says:)

CHIEF BROWN BEAR

Me pray to Great Sky Spirit.

BILLY

Oh, I'm sorry, Chief. I'll wait inside until the service is over.

CHIEF BROWN BEAR

Me finish.

BILLY

To tell you the truth, Chief, I'm kind of glad I ran into you.
(Sitting at L. of him)
I thought you might be able to fix me up with an Indian suit.

CHIEF BROWN BEAR

Me ask Great Sky Spirit if me should make you my son.

BILLY

Your son? What'd he have to say?

CHIEF BROWN BEAR

Great Sky Spirit say yes. Great Sky Spirit say good for Kadota future. Me hope real son carry on tradition of Kodota Tribe but real son die hero; go Happy Hunting Ground.

BILLY

Gee, that's too bad, Chief; that'll make two of us right in a row.

CHIEF BROWN BEAR

Two?

BILLY

I may have to go on a little mission tonight. Nothing much; I just won't get back alive

CHIEF BROWN BEAR

You be safe. Me give charms.

BILLY

Charms?

CHIEF BROWN BEAR

And me give you Indian buckskins fit for son of Chief. Come to teepee when moon come over mountain. We have ceremony. There you become my dead son re-born. Me give you *his* Indian dress to wear. *You* become Yellow Feather!

BILLY

Yellow Feather. Say, I like that. Well, I'll see you tonight, Chief.
(Starts to exit R., then turns and raises his hand)
Dakota.

CHIEF BROWN BEAR

(Correcting him)
Ka-doe-ta!

BILLY

Ka-doe-ta. Yeh, that's better: Ka-doe-ta!
(BILLY exits R. CHIEF BROWN BEAR puts his ear to the ground and YELLOW FEATHER'S call is heard faintly from off-stage. LITTLE MARY enters from the Inn carrying an Indian blanket. CHIEF BROWN BEAR sits erect upon hearing her enter)

LITTLE MARY

(Placing blanket around his shoulders)
Here, Indian Father; the evening chill is already in the air. Are you sure you won't sleep in the Inn tonight?

CHIEF BROWN BEAR

Me sleep in teepee many years. No cold. No ache. No pain. White Man have all. Why two Indians here?

LITTLE MARY

Two Indians? You must be mistaken, Indian Father.

CHIEF BROWN BEAR

No mistake. Two Indians here.

LITTLE MARY

Oh, yes, now that you mention it, there was an Indian here. An Indian guide came to take Captain Jim on a mission.

CHIEF BROWN BEAR

And other?

LITTLE MARY

No other.

CHIEF BROWN BEAR

(Rises slowly)
Yes. Other Indian here. Me know! Me feel!
(Xing to exit U.C., then turning back)
Is very still. Is too still. Bad sign. If bad happen, Merry Sunshine, run faster than wind to teepee of Indian Father.
(Raising arm)
Kadota!

LITTLE MARY

Kadota, Indian Father.

(CHIEF BROWN BEAR exits U.R. LITTLE MARY, in a state, crosses U.L. and leans on the porch rail. YELLOW FEATHER's call is heard. Reacting to the "call" LITTLE MARY wheels around and dashes D.L. just in time to be startled by ERNESTINE VON LIEBEDICH entering R.)

LITTLE MARY

Oh, Madame Ernestine! You gave me a start.

ERNESTINE

(Xing L. to Little Mary)
Vas iss los? Vas iss los?

LITTLE MARY

(Xing R. and below Ernestine)
It's, it's nothing, Madame Ernestine.

ERNESTINE

Ya, iss somting. You shiffer und shake. Come, liebchen; tell.

LITTLE MARY

Oh, Madame Ernestine, Captain Jim is on the trail of Yellow Feather, a savage Indian I had long thought dead.
(Xing U.R. and looking off-R.)
Yellow Feather will stop at nothing.
(Xing D.L. to Ernestine)
I'm so frightened for the Captain and, oh, Madame, I'm frightened for myself.

ERNESTINE

For self, liebchen?

LITTLE MARY

Yellow Feather has sworn revenge on me.
(Xing D.L. below Ernestine)
He threatened that one day he would return and, and have his way with me.

ERNESTINE

There, there, mine liebchen. Calm, calm. Der past iss in der past; and der present? Der present iss only as ve see it; und so ve must make der present as pleasant as ve may:
(Music in: EVERY LITTLE NOTHING. Helping LITTLE MARY to the bench, ERNESTINE stands behind her and sings:)

EVERY LITTLE NOTHING
(Means a Precious Little Nothing)
(MME. ERNESTINE and LITTLE MARY)

Refrain
ERNESTINE

> Effry little nutting
> > Meance a precious little nutting
> > > If ve make it gay
> Effry little nutting
> > Meance a precious little nutting
> > > But it cannot schtay
> For effry little moment
> > Hass its moment
> > > Den it flice avay
> Effry little nutting
> > Meance a precious little nutting
> > > Take it vile you may.

— 32 —

ERNESTINE (con't.)

*(Cheered by Mme. Ernestine's words of wisdom, LITTLE MARY joins
her in the second refrain; LITTLE MARY singing the melody,
ERNESTINE the contralto harmony. THEY gracefully cross ard
re-cross the stage as they sing)*

ERNESTINE &
LITTLE MARY   Every little nothing
                Means a precious little nothing
                    If we make it gay
                Every little nothing
                Means a precious little nothing
                    But it cannot stay
              For every little moment
                Has its moment
                  Then it flies away
              Every little nothing
                Means a precious little nothing
                Take it while you may.

*(At the end of the refrain MME. ERNESTINE places a wisp of nothing
in LITTLE MARY's cupped hands. Little Mary holds it in front of
her, opens her hands, and blows it away. The two wave goodbye to
it. During the rest of the first half of the third refrain THEY do a
carefree dance, then once more join in harmony and sing:)*

ERNESTINE &
LITTLE MARY   For every little moment
                Has its moment
                  Then it flies away
              Every little nothing
                Means a precious little nothing
                Take it while you may

*(THEY tenderly end the number C., LITTLE MARY nestled in
ERNESTINE's arms. LITTLE MARY (and the audience) are in a
position to see a tall, yellow feather appear over the top of the
wall. YELLOW FEATHER's call is heard as LITTLE MARY
screams:)*

LITTLE MARY

(Xing to wall; then to porch rail)
Yellow Feather! Yellow Feather!

ERNESTINE

(Xing to her)
Vas iss los, mine liebchen, vas iss los?

LITTLE MARY

I saw it, Madame Ernestine, I saw it: a yellow feather, a bright yellow
feather coming over the wall!

ERNESTINE

Dere, dere; you iss overwrought. Come, liebchen, ve no alarm der others.
Ve vill go to der Inn.

(The Inn door opens a crack)
Och; iss too late. Day come. Do not fret: Madame Ernestine explain avay
effryting. Come; ve sit like nutting happen.

(MME. ERNESTINE and LITTLE MARY sit on bench D.R.)
(Music in, FINALE ACT I)

FINALE, ACT I

*(LITTLE MARY, NANCY, ERNESTINE, YOUNG LADIES and
FOREST RANGERS)*
*(Music mysterioso. Led by NANCY, the FOREST RANGERS and
YOUNG LADIES (ENSEMBLE) enter cautiously on tiptoe)*

ENSEMBLE
Final Chorus   What has happened?
                                  What has happened?
                                     Tell us now without delay
                                  What has happened?
                                  What has happened?
                                     Tell us, tell us right away
                                  What has happened?
                                     We can scarcely wait
                                  What has happened?
                                     Please don't hesitate

Chorale   Don't keep us in suspense
                                  Our interest is intense
                                  Don't keep us in suspense,
                                  Don't keep us in suspense,
                                     Don't keep us,
                                     Don't keep us,
                                     Don't keep us,
                                  Don't keep us in suspense
                                  Because our int'rest is intense
                                  Please tell us what has happened
                                     Tell us now
                                  Yes, tell us what has happened
                                     Tell us now
                                  Who can solve the mystery?
                                  Tell us right away for we
                                  Cannot contain ourselves
                                  One single moment longer:
                                  What has happened?

Recitative
ERNESTINE   Nothing that concerns you has happened;
                                  Nothing that concerns you has taken place!

ENSEMBLE   Nothing that concerns us has happened;
                                  Nothing that concerns us has taken place!

NANCY   Has anything that doesn't concern us happened?
                                  Has anything that doesn't concern us taken place?

ENSEMBLE   Has anything that doesn't concern us happened?
                                  Has anything that doesn't concern us taken place?

LITTLE MARY   Yes, yes, my friends; yes, yes, I must confess
                                     For I can feel your deep devotion
                                  With blushing face I deign to answer yes:
                                     It has to do with my emotion

ENSEMBLE   Dear me, dear me; you say that you
                                     Are blushing; dear, . . . we're blushing, too

Aria
LITTLE MARY   Please forgive me if my leave I'm taking
                                     I must find an answer to my fears:
                                  When I feel my lonely heart is breaking
                                     How can I go smiling through my tears?

ENSEMBLE   We forgive you if your leave you're taking
                                     You must find an answer to your fears:
                                  When you feel your lonely heart is breaking
                                     How can you go smiling through your tears?

*(LITTLE MARY walks slowly, but nobly, towards the Inn door as the
ENSEMBLE looks on; then:)*

— 34 —

ENSEMBLE	You've told us how

LITTLE MARY
(Turning back)
I've told you how?

ENSEMBLE Yes, this we vow

LITTLE MARY Then tell me now
Refrain

ENSEMBLE When e'er a cloud appears
Filled with doubt and fears
Look for a sky of blue
When e'er a cloud of grey
Seems to waft your way
Look for a sky of biue

LITTLE MARY I must remember
The sun is shining
It may be shining,
Some day for me, ...

(The ORCHESTRA takes over the melody as LITTLE MARY breaks down. In tears she goes to ERNESTINE's arms for comfort)

ENSEMBLE So 'til that happy day
YOU must learn to say
Look for a sky of blue.

(Unbeknownst to LITTLE MARY and the ENSEMBLE, we see YELLOW FEATHER, tomahawk in hand, standing on the garden wall; in all his menacing, savage glory. Wild Indian music is heard as:)
(THE CURTAIN FALLS)
(THE CURTAIN RISES AGAIN FOR TABLEAU)
(THE CURTAIN FALLS)

Act II

SCENE 1

The Garden. It is now gaily decorated with lanterns. There is a serving table in front of the tree U.R. The YOUNG LADIES and FOREST RANGERS are discovered dancing to and talking over the happy waltz music that has opened the scene. They come forward and sing:
SUCH A MERRY PARTY
(OPENING CHORUS, ACT II)
(NANCY, FOREST RANGERS & YOUNG LADIES)

1st Refrain
FOREST RANGERS
& YOUNG LADIES
Ha, ha: ho, ho:
Such a merry party
Ha, ha; it's so gay
And the jolliest jesting one hears
Ever after
The laughter

FOREST RANGERS & YOUNG LADIES (con't.)
Will ring in my ears
With its ha, ha; ho, ho:
Such a merry party
It's so filled with mirth;
It's the veriest airiest, merriest party
The merriest party on earth:
Ha, ha!
(NANCY enters U.L. and passes among the guests collecting empty glasses from them)

Interlude

RANGERS	It's lots of fun with lots of eats
NANCY	And lots of men
LADIES	There's pots of dainty little sweets
	And pots of men
RANGERS	We like the drinks a man can swill
NANCY	I like the men
LADIES	We love the fuss and love the frill
NANCY	I love the men
RANGERS	There's lots of the liquid that mellows
NANCY	There's lots of fellows
LADIES	So many dear favors and caps
NANCY	So many chaps
RANGERS	And one or two make a man tingle
NANCY	And they're all single
LADIES	A party can make a girl dream of romance
RANGERS	Shall we dance?
LADIES & RANGERS	Then perchance
	We shall do more than dream of romance!
NANCY	There's lots of pants!

(NANCY exits U.L., dancing)

2nd Refrain
FOREST RANGERS
& YOUNG LADIES
Ha, ha; ho, ho:
Such a merry party
Ha, ha; it's so gay
And the jolliest jesting one hears
Ever after
The laughter
Will ring in my ears
With its ha, ha; ho, ho:
Such a merry party,
It's so filled with mirth
It's the veriest airiest, merriest party
The merriest party on earth:
Ha, ha!

(After the Opening Chorus, the FOREST RANGERS and YOUNG LADIES retire to the background and "dumb show" party behavior. They exit in pairs during the following scene.
NANCY enters U.L. and crosses to C. where she spies BILLY (who has entered during the Opening Chorus) sitting on the porch steps)

NANCY

(Xing to Billy)
Hello, Billy. Enjoying the party?

BILLY

It's difficult for one to enjoy the frivolities of life when one is staring death in the face. But then, you seem to be making up for both of us.

NANCY

But isn't that what a party's for? To have fun?

BILLY

Oh, yes, yes. Indeed it is.
(Rising and crossing C.)
You go right ahead and have your fun with all those other men while I go risk my life on a secret mission.

NANCY

(Xing to Billy)
A secret mission? Doing what?

BILLY

That's what's secret about it. I, I probably shan't come back, you know.

NANCY

Well, if you're not coming back why can't you tell me?

BILLY

I'll tell you this much: if you meet a mysterious Indian tonight, don't scream; it's me.

NANCY

Oh, disguises. I just love disguises.

BILLY

I guess this is it, old girl. If I return, I shall make you mine and if I don't, well, I want you to have this.

NANCY

Oh, Billy!
(Surprised)
A pawn ticket?

BILLY

It's on my grandmother's wedding ring.

NANCY

It's — it's lovely, Billy.

BILLY

Chin up, old girl, and put 'er there.
(Shakes hands)

NANCY

Goodbye, Billy. You take good care of yourself now.

BILLY

Don't worry about me, old girl; I know where I'm going.
> (*Turning dramatically, he bumps headlong into MABEL and spills crumb cake on her*)

Oh, I'm terribly sorry. How clumsy of me. Do excuse me.
> (*Tries to brush her off*)

Here. No. It was, — well, goodbye.
> (*BILLY rapidly exits R. and MABEL exits, smilingly distraught, into the Inn*)

NANCY

This is the first present he ever gave me. He must be getting serious.
> (*NANCY exits D.L. as the YOUNG LADIES enter from U.L. and come D.C.*)

CORA

I do hope dear Little Mary's emotional condition is better.

MAUD

The poor thing. She was shaken up, wasn't she?

GWENDOLYN

And did you notice how pale and drawn she looks this evening?

BLANCH

I was surprised the poor dear came down to the party at all.
> (*HENRIETTA opens Inn door, sees LITTLE MARY approaching, and quickly crosses down to the YOUNG LADIES*)

HENRIETTA

Shhh. Don't say another word. Here she comes now.

GWENDOLYN

We must act as if nothing has happened.
> (*LITTLE MARY enters from the Inn and addresses the Young Ladies from the porch:*)

LITTLE MARY

Good evening girls. I do hope you're having a pleasant time.

CORA

> (*Xing to porch rail*)

Never mind us, you poor thing, you.

MAUD

It's perfectly terrible what's happened to you.

GWENDOLYN

And we're dreadfully upset for you.

LITTLE MARY

> (*Xing D.L.*)

I'm quite all right now, thank you.

MAUD

How brave of you.

BLANCH

The courage of you Western women!

GWENDOLYN

I'm sure *I* could never be so composed if *my* fiance had left on some unknown, dangerous mission.

HENRIETTA

Probably *never* to return.

LITTLE MARY

(Xing to C.)
I'm sure he'll be back later this evening.

MAUD

We're *awfully* glad for your sake *you're* so sure.

CORA

But if he *shouldn't* return — — —

GWENDOLYN

Feel free to call on us.

HENRIETTA

We'll cheer you up, dear.

LITTLE MARY

(Xing to Inn steps)
Thank you. I do appreciate your kindness.
(An auto horn is heard)
(The YOUNG LADIES peer off U.R.)

CORA

What ever could that be? It sounds like an auto touring car.

MAUD

It looks like an auto touring car.

GWENDOLYN

It is an auto touring car.

HENRIETTA

What ever would an auto touring car be doing way up here in this wild territory?

LITTLE MARY

It must be my dear friend, General Oscar Fairfax.

YOUNG LADIES

(Primping)
General!

LITTLE MARY

Retired.

YOUNG LADIES

(Disappointed)
Oh.

MARY

He's awaiting his appointment as United States Ambassador to France.

YOUNG LADIES

(Primping)
Ambassador to France?

LITTLE MARY

Meanwhile he's been appointed Temporary Assistant Under-Secretary, Second in Charge of Indian Affairs.

— 39 —

YOUNG LADIES

(Disappointed)

Oh.

GWENDOLYN

(Xing D.L.)

Might he be one of the Fairfaxes from Philadelphia?

LITTLE MARY

I believe he does come from there.

YOUNG LADIES

(Primping)

Oh, la! A Philadelphia Fairfax!

(The FOREST RANGERS re-enter from various entrances and the YOUNG LADIES rejoin their partners. NANCY enters U.R., speaking to OSCAR FAIRFAX who is off — U.R.)

NANCY

Oh, General, you're such a tease.

(Gaining control of herself NANCY makes a formal announcement)

General Oscar Fairfax.

(GENERAL OSCAR FAIRFAX enters U.R. and crosses to Little Mary)

OSCAR

Ah, my own Little Mary. Let me look at you.

(Surveying the party)

Well, well, well, what's going on?

LITTLE MARY

A garden party, General, and you're just in time.

(NANCY takes the jewel case OSCAR is carrying, along with his hat, goggles, and gloves)

OSCAR

Thank you, my dear. Yes, Nancy Twinkle, you *are* getting prettier every time I see you.

NANCY

Thank you, General.

(NANCY leaves jewel case on tree stump U.C. and exits U.L.)

LITTLE MARY

And what brings you to the Colorado Inn at this time of night, General?

OSCAR

Business, my dear.

(Looking over the Young Ladies)

Unfortunately, business. I was at Forest Ranger Headquarters this afternoon and they thought Troup Fourteen should have arrived at your Inn by today. Have you seen anything of them?

LITTLE MARY

Why; why, they're right here, General.

OSCAR

(Looking around)

Well, so they are. Couldn't see the Forest Rangers for the limbs, so to speak. Yes, yes, yes. Well, now then, I must see Captain Warington at once.

LITTLE MARY

Captain Warington is on a special mission. We expect him back later this evening.

OSCAR

But this is of the utmost importance. Now tell me, who's second in command?

LITTLE MARY

Poor Sergeant McGinty, but he's confined to Headquarters Hospital.

OSCAR

Well, somebody must be in charge.

LITTLE MARY

That would be Corporal Jester, but I'm afraid he's been sent on a mission, too.

OSCAR

I should think they'd have more sense than to leave when I'm coming. You, there.
(PETE, a Private First Class, steps forward)

PETE

Yes, Sir?

OSCAR

Well, Private, it looks as if you're the ranking officer around here.

PETE

Yes, Sir.

OSCAR

I have authority from Ranger Headquarters to have your troop placed at my disposal. You and your men must find Captain Warington at all costs. You do a good job and I shall recommend you for a promotion.

PETE

Yes, Sir. Thank you, Sir.
(PETE blows whistle and the FOREST RANGERS assemble)

OSCAR

My dear, I am sorry to disrupt your party this way, but it's most urgent that Captain Warington be found.

LITTLE MARY

God bless you, General Fairfax. You're a heaven-sent angel.

PETE

(To assembled Forest Rangers)
Into your battle dress, men, and on your return I shall split the troop into search parties. Troop, dismissed!
(The FOREST RANGERS rush off U.L. and the dismayed YOUNG LADIES cluster around OSCAR)

GWENDOLYN

(Kneeling)
Oh, General Fairfax, . . .

OSCAR

Well, well, well; what have we here?

HENRIETTA

Will they be gone long?

OSCAR

(Taking her hand)
Not long enough, I'm afraid; not long enough.

MAUD

(Kneeling)
Oh, General, will it be dangerous?

OSCAR

Reasonably so, my dear; reasonably so.

CORA

What ever shall we do?

OSCAR

There, there, there; don't you worry your pretty little head about that.
Uncle Oscar will keep you amused.

YOUNG LADIES

Uncle Oscar?

OSCAR

Yes; I want you all to look on me as your dear Uncle Oscar.
    (OSCAR spies MABEL standing D.R.)
And what might *your* name be?
    (OSCAR crosses to MABEL and she smiles)

GWENDOLYN

That's Mabel.

BLANCH

Mabel doesn't say very much.

OSCAR

Mabel, you're the smartest female I ever met. Now, would you be kind
enough to fetch me my goodie box?

YOUNG LADIES

A goodie box? What ever is a goodie box?
    (MABEL goes U.C. and gets jewel box)

OSCAR

A goodie box is a box filled with all manner of goodies that little girls love.
You see I'm very fond of giving things away; particularly to little girls.
    (MABEL hands him the box)
Thank you, my dear. You did that very well; very well indeed.
    (Looking in box)
Now, let me see; ah, just the thing. One for you,
    *(He hands a necklace to MABEL. She holds it around her neck and
        smiles. The other YOUNG LADIES gasp)*
And one for you,
    (He puts a bracelet around GWENDOLYN's arm)

GWENDOLYN

Oh, Uncle Oscar, it's beautiful!
    *(OSCAR gives bracelets to HENRIETTA and BLANCH and they
        gaze at the gifts in ecstasy)*

OSCAR

And I have just the one for you;
    (He takes out a brooch for MAUD)
But you must let *me* pin it on.
    (He starts to do so)

CORA

Girls, give the presents back.

— 42 —

Give the presents back?

CORA

Young ladies from Eastchester Finishing School cannot accept gifts from a single gentleman.

OSCAR

Oh, but my dear, I've *been* married; several times.

CORA

Even so, it isn't proper.

OSCAR

Oh, but it is. Remember, for all practical purposes, I'm your dear, old Uncle Oscar; an intimate member of the family, so to speak.

(Music in, "SAY UNCLE." The Verse is almost spoken by OSCAR)
SAY "UNCLE"
(GENERAL OSCAR FAIRFAX and YOUNG LADIES)

Verse
OSCAR

There's a saying that it's better
If we give than if we take
And I want to give but etiquette says
no;
I can't carry out its letter
And its form I must forsake
But I've kept the spirit proper as I'll show:
And so:

1st Refrain

Think of me as a kind and loving uncle
Uncle is just the thing I want to be
You're my very fav'rite nieces
That I simply love to pieces
Won't you come and sit on Uncle's knee?
You dimpled darlings,
Uncle can give you lots of pretty presents
Uncle is not a kith, he's just a kin
Take them please
Or I must squeeze
Your dainty hands 'til you all, say "Uncle"

YOUNG LADIES   Say "Uncle"

OSCAR   Say, "Uncle"; Uncle, dear, you win

YOUNG LADIES   Say "Uncle"?

OSCAR   Yes, "Uncle"

ALL   Say, "Uncle"; Uncle, dear, you win.

2nd Refrain
*(During the second refrain THEY dance. As OSCAR chucks MABEL
    under the chin HE sings:)*

OSCAR   Oh, joy, delicious . . .
(After dance)

Interlude
YOUNG LADIES   'Though returning gifts is very impolite
We are not convinced that what we've done is right
Innocent it seems to us; but is it quite?
So tell us once again
The charming theory you ascertain.

3rd Refrain

OSCAR

  Think of me as a kind and loving Uncle
  Giving a trinket here, a bauble there
  I am like the baby brother
  Of your darling Dad and Mother
  Let me run my fingers through your hair,
    You'll learn to love it,
  Uncle delights in giving pretty playthings
  Tell me that not my bounds I've overstepped
    Take my gold
    Or I must hold
  You tightly, dears, 'til you all

OSCAR   Say "Uncle"

YOUNG LADIES   Say, "Uncle"?

OSCAR   Say, "Uncle; Uncle, I accept"

YOUNG LADIES   Say, "Uncle"?

OSCAR   Yes, "Uncle"

ALL   Oh, (Say) Uncle I accept.
  *(At the end of the number the YOUNG LADIES huddle together for
  a moment, then turn to OSCAR)*

                    YOUNG LADIES
We've decided to accept your gifts.

                         CORA
That is, if our husbands-to-be don't object.

                        OSCAR
Husbands-to-be?

                         MAUD
We became engaged to the Forest Rangers this very afternoon.

                      GWENDOLYN
Do you think they'll object?

                        OSCAR
Object? If they don't object, you should call the engagement off.
  (Collecting gifts from YOUNG LADIES)
Under the circumstances, my conduct has been highly improper. Highly
improper. To think that I, Oscar Fairfax of the Philadelphia Fairfaxes, tried
to force my gifts on Young Ladies who are in a highly advanced state of
betrothal. If I were your intended, I'd horsewhip me, that's what I'd do;
horsewhip me. Ah, Mabel, to think what we might have been to one another.
  *(Starts to take necklace from MABEL. There is a small tug-of-war.
  MABEL smiles and OSCAR, taken in, places the necklace back
  around her neck)*
Oh, well, my dear; keep smiling.
  (Kisses her on the cheek and exits D.L.)
  *(Trumpet Call. The FOREST RANGERS, now dressed in "battle
  dress", enter U.L. Over the battle call they bid a hasty farewell to
  the YOUNG LADIES, then line up down across the front of the
  stage. The YOUNG LADIES remain in the background, waving
  goodbye, as the Point Look-Out drop flies in)*

Act II

Point Look-Out.
The drop is in back of the FOREST RANGERS and in
front of the YOUNG LADIES. PETE assembles the
FOREST RANGERS:

PETE

Troop 'Tention!
Gentlemen: I want half of you to surround the Inn,
    (Points off D.R.)
and protect the ladies from any dangers that may arise.
The other half will follow me.
    (Points off D.L.)
To danger, and possible death. Salute one. Ho!
    (Music in, Reprise, "THE FOREST RANGER".)

REPRISE
THE FOREST RANGER
(FOREST RANGERS)

FOREST RANGERS
Refrain   Stout hearted is the Forest Ranger
                            He's a scout
                     He's thoughtful, friendly, courteous and kind
                            He's reverent and grave
                            He's healthy and he's brave
                     He's clean in soul and body and mind
                            Yes, sir!
                     He's cheerful, honest, thrifty and obedient
                     To love the good and hate the bad is his plan
                            So if there's any danger
                            You can be sure the Forest Ranger
                     Ever will march on man to man.
                     To man to man to man to man.
        (All the FOREST RANGERS march out D.R. at
                        BLACKOUT)

Act II

SCENE 3

In front of Chief Brown Bear's Teepee (Set-piece with
flap, in front of Point Look-Out drop). The following
dialogue is heard during the BLACKOUT:

CHIEF BROWN BEAR

Ya too ho kee ton go la.

BILLY

Ho kee ton go la.

CHIEF BROWN BEAR

Say hay kee tow.

BILLY

Say hay kee tow.

CHIEF BROWN BEAR

Ra hoe may, day da ka doe ka.

BILLY

What?

CHIEF BROWN BEAR

Ra hoe may, day da ka doe ka.

BILLY

Ra hoe may, day da ka doe ka.

CHIEF BROWN BEAR

Shaun te Kadota.

BILLY

Shaun te Kadota.

CHIEF BROWN BEAR

Pong!

BILLY

Pong!

(The lights come up and BILLY is seen coming out of the Teepee dressed in an Indian suit. He is followed by CHIEF BROWN BEAR)

BILLY

(Wiping brow and coughing)

Ah, fresh air. Your Teepee's a little stuffy, Chief. Tell me, do you always keep your horse in there with you?

CHIEF BROWN BEAR

Indian pony's good animal. He like me. He like you, too.

BILLY

Well, as long as he likes us, that makes all the difference. Yes, sir, that was quite a ceremony, Chief, quite a ceremony. I feel like an Indian already.

(Assuming Indian pose)

How's this?

CHIEF BROWN BEAR

You *are* Indian. You Kadota. Now me make you man.

BILLY

Oh?

CHIEF BROWN BEAR

I give you wisdom, I make you have courage, I bring you manly streng

BILLY

You don't say?

CHIEF BROWN BEAR

Sit!

(BILLY sits on rock L. of C.)

CHIEF BROWN BEAR

(Blessing food)

Do hot do aye ah too. Do hot do aye ah too. For wisdom. Eat.

BILLY

Humm. That's very taste. Very tasty indeed.

CHIEF BROWN BEAR

Eagle brain. Do hot do aye ah too. Do hot do aye ah too. For coura

BILLY

It's kind of gooey. My, oh, my. Yes, sir. What was it?

CHIEF BROWN BEAR

Mountain lion eyes. Do hot do aye ah too. Do hot do aye ah too. For
manly strength. Eat.

BILLY

I'm not very hungry. It's, it's very, . . . what is it? On second thought,
don't tell me.

CHIEF BROWN BEAR

Wash down with Fire Water.
(Hands him skin bag)

BILLY

Say, Chief, that's very, . . .
(Stomps around)
Ooo whee! Ooo whee!

CHIEF BROWN BEAR

(Pleased)
You make fine Indian dancer. You man now. You my son. Now me give
you presents.

BILLY

Chief, if you're not careful you're going to kill me with kindness.

CHIEF BROWN BEAR

First, feather.
(Sticks feather in BILLY's head band)
Yellow feather for Yellow Feather.

BILLY

There you go getting clever again.

CHIEF BROWN BEAR

Indian belt.

BILLY

Say, Chief, this is really something. What are all the little furry things?

CHIEF BROWN BEAR

White man scalps. Best present last. Bow and arrow. Me have many, many
years. Very fine.

BILLY

Oh, Chief, I couldn't take that. Really.

CHIEF BROWN BEAR

You take. You my son now.

BILLY

Gee, this is a jim dandy.
(Tries it out. Shoots arrow off-stage)
My gosh; I didn't know it was loaded. You'd better teach me how to use
this thing.

CHIEF BROWN BEAR

Tomorrow. Tomorrow me teach. Me teach you ride Indian pony, too.
Bareback.

BILLY

Bareback? Now wait a minute, Chief . . . .

Tonight, tonight me pray to Great Sky Spirit. I thank Great Sky Spirit for bringing me son.

BILLY

Hey, look, Chief; I brought you some presents, too. Here; first, a pocket knife.

CHIEF BROWN BEAR

Poc-ket knife?

BILLY

Yea, for cutting. Very handy.
(Demonstrates)
You can use it for all sorts of things: eat with it, screw driver, clean your nails; oh, it has all kinds of uses. Then, let's see; Oh, yes, a copy of the Rules and Regulations for a Forest Ranger. That's the best companion a man ever had.
(CHIEF BROWN BEAR nods appreciatively as he reads it up-side-down. BILLY rights it)

BILLY

Now, one more. Ah, yes. Necktie.
(Displays a bright necktie)

CHIEF BROWN BEAR

(Looks quizzically at necktie)
Neck-tie?

BILLY

(Putting necktie around CHIEF BROWN BEAR's neck)
You wear it around your neck. And what it does; it sort of gives you that, that dressed up look.

CHIEF BROWN BEAR

My son give me presents. My son give me neck-tie. Very good son. Me wear neck-tie, always.

BILLY

It look good. Me like. Me like? Now you've got me talking that way.

CHIEF BROWN BEAR

(Sitting on rock)
Eagle brain take effect. Me glad.

BILLY

You know what, Chief; me glad, too.
(Music in, ME, A HEAP BIG INJUN. The song is sung and danced by BILLY as CHIEF BROWN BEAR watches and beats the rhythm on a small tom-tom)

ME A HEAP BIG INJUN
(BILLY)

BILLY
1st Refrain

Me a heap big Injun
Me a big Kadota Injun through and through
A feather in my hat I couldn't weather
But now I wear a hat in my feather
Me a heap big Injun
And we heap big Injuns know a thing or two
We have a special language that I only mastered now:
Instead of saying "how d'ya do" we Injuns just say "How";
Oh, me a big Kadota
Me a heap big Injun through and through.

When I was but a lad of five
I dreamed that I would be
An Injun Brave who lived inside a Tee-Pee
My dreams have all come true at last,
'Though I am over five
And I will be the finest Brave alive;
I've
Always been a Pale Face, born and bred,
But since I . . .   the change is my face Red:
It's gotta be said,
That,

2nd Refrain   Me a heap big Injun
Me a Big Kadota Injun through and through
Not long ago I couldn't hold my liquor
Now Fire Water makes me even sicker
Me a heap big Injun
And we heap big Injuns know a thing or two
From the saddle I would always fall off horses I recall
But I'll soon be riding bareback 'cause there's not so far to fall
Oh, me a big Kadota
Me a heap big Injun through and through.

3rd Refrain
(During the first half of this Refrain BILLY does an Indian Dance)
Me a heap big Injun
And we heap big Injuns know a squaw or two
I'll have a laugh with Minnie-ha-ha, Pretty Red Wing I'll reform
I'll lose my head for Pocohontas if she'll keep my wigwam warm:
Oh, me a big Kadota
Me a heap big Injun through and through:
HOW!
BLACKOUT

Act II

SCENE 4

*CORA'S bedroom. There is a large bed U.C. and two
windows, one U.L. and one L. There is a screen D.L. and
a chest D.R. As the lights come up a chime strikes ten
o'clock. A tick-tock sound is heard from the orchestra.
The YOUNG LADIES, now dressed in nightgowns, are
discovered grouped around the stage in attractive poses.
Simultaneously they sigh very deeply and change their
poses.*

CORA

How very quiet it is.

MAUD

And how very sad.

GWENDOLYN

Even poor Mabel finds it difficult to smile, don't you, Mabel?
(*MABEL forces a smile as she dabs an eye with the front of her
nightgown*)

HENRIETTA

Perhaps we shouldn't have left the party.

GWENDOLYN

How can you feel like a party, dear? Your loved one has left your side.

HENRIETTA

Who?

CORA

Your loved one, dear. Your husband-to-be.

HENRIETTA

Oh, yes, I almost forgot.
(NANCY enters U.C., crosses below bed and to window U.L.)

NANCY

S'cuse me, girls.

MAUD

For goodness sake, what ever are you doing?

NANCY

I'm making my escape.

GWENDOLYN

Your escape from where?

NANCY

From here.

BLANCH

Why don't you use the front door?

NANCY

I don't want anyone to see me.

BLANCH

Oh.

NANCY

(Crossing to chest D.R.)
Something very mysterious is going on out there, and I'm going to find out what it is. All I need is a suitable disguise.
(NANCY searches through chest)

GWENDOLYN

Are you *really* going out there?

NANCY

Of course I am. I'm going out and help Billy. Do you want to come along?

YOUNG LADIES

Dear me, no.

GWENDOLYN

Just think what might happen to a girl.

NANCY

That's what I've been thinking about.
(Gathering up costume)
There. I guess I've got everything I'm going to need.

BLANCH

Oh, Nancy, you make sin sound like such *fun*.

NANCY

(Crossing to screen)
Well, I certainly wouldn't want to be a corrupting influence.
(Holds out pack of cigarettes)
Fatima, anyone?
*(NANCY exits behind screen as LITTLE MARY enters U.C. with
lighted candle)*

LITTLE MARY

Good gracious me. I should have thought by this time you young ladies
would have been fast asleep in your little trundles.

GWENDOLYN

It's very difficult when our loved ones, our husbands-to-be, have left
our sides.

CORA

Probably never to return.

MAUD

We're hoping for a piece of news.

HENRIETTA

One way or the other.

BLANCH

Nancy's going into the night to find out all about it.

LITTLE MARY

Nancy? Nancy, are you hiding behind that screen?
(NANCY throws dress over screen)
Oh, Nancy, whatever are we going to do with you?

We can't condone your headstrong way
And yet you make our lives so gay.
*(Music in, NAUGHTY NAUGHTY NANCY, as LITTLE MARY
sits on the bed with the YOUNG LADIES)*
NAUGHTY, NAUGHTY NANCY
(LITTLE MARY and YOUNG LADIES)

Refrain

LITTLE MARY   Naughty, Naughty Nancy, you're so mischievous, it's true:
You're so full of ginger and so full of spice;
We can't help but wonder how a naughty girl like you
Can be so naughty yet so very nice;
Ever laughing, ever chaffing
Filled with glee
Ever joking, ever poking
Fun at ev-ry one you see; so
Naughty, Naughty Nancy, you're a caution, yes you are;
You're a caution yet we love the things you do
There are even times we wish we would and wish we could
Be Naughty, Naughty Nancys, too!

Interlude

LITTLE MARY
&
YOUNG LADIES   Running hither, running thither,
Running, running, who knows whither,
Running to and fro and all around;
Running here and running there and
Running, running ev'rywhere, you're
Running ev'rywhere but running down

LITTLE MARY   We are quite afraid you'll catch a chill
For you're like an effervescent, bubbly glass
Of Sa's' —
Parill . . . a,

— 51 —

LITTLE MARY   Naughty, Naughty Nancy, you're a caution, yes you are;
&   You're a caution yet we love the things you do
YOUNG LADIES There are even times we wish we would and wish we could
              Be Naughty, Naughty Nancys, too.

LITTLE MARY *(Spoken)* Now Nancy you behave!
    (LITTLE MARY exits U.C. at end of song)
    (After the song NANCY comes from behind the screen dressed in a long, black cape. She wears a black band around her forehead. The YOUNG LADIES gasp, more in delight than horror)

NANCY
(Crossing D.R.)
Do you think I look mysterious enough?

MAUD
Oh, Nancy, it's a wonderful disguise.

NANCY
Do I look seductive and beautiful?

HENRIETTA
Oh, yes! We'd never have known it was you.

GWENDOLYN
Who are you disguised as?

NANCY
Oh, this isn't the real disguise. This just disguises the disguise I'm going to have on underneath.

GWENDOLYN
Oh.

NANCY
That's the way Mata Hari did it.

YOUNG LADIES
Who?

NANCY
Mata Hari. I read all about her in the Penny Dreadfuls.

BLANCH
Penny Dreadfuls? Do you read Penny Dreadfuls?

NANCY
Oh, yes, all the time; but Mata Hari's my favorite. I'm practically an authority on her.

GWENDOLYN
You don't mean it.

NANCY
Oh, yes; a real authority.

CORA
How shocking.

HENRIETTA
Tell us about her.
    (NANCY moves up and sits on the bed. The YOUNG LADIES crowd around her)

NANCY

Well, I suppose Mata Hari was just about the wickedest woman in the whole world. She was a spy by trade, you know.

GWENDOLYN

A spy. How exciting.

HENRIETTA

I wish I could be a spy.

NANCY

Well . . . she spied differently than most spies spy.

CORA

How's that?

NANCY

Well, you see, first she made all the men fall madly in love with her and then she'd cast them aside like an old pair of shoes as soon as she got what she wanted out of them.

HENRIETTA

What did she want?

NANCY

Well, they never explained that part too well, but I must say, . . . she certainly did get results!

> (Music in, MATA HARI, sung by NANCY and the YOUNG LADIES. NANCY almost speaks the Verses and conducts it like a Cheer Leader leading a yell)

MATA HARI
(NANCY and YOUNG LADIES)

Verse

NANCY — Who's the girl who had the men all eating from her hand?

YOUNG LADIES — Mata Hari, Mata Hari

NANCY — Who could turn a passing whim into a stern command?
YOUNG LADIES — Mata Hari, Mata Hari
NANCY — Who would spy and get her data
By doing this and that-a?

YOUNG LADIES — Mata!

Refrain
YOUNG LADIES — Mata Hari, Mata Hari,
Oh, what a wicked girl was she
That's the kind of girl I'll never be
Mata Hari, Mata Hari,
That's the kind of wicked girl I'll never be.

Interlude
NANCY — Mata Hari had a very wicked reputation
She was willing to be thrilling for her information
She would weave her magic spell
Then she'd make them kiss and tell
For her the men all had a yen yet Mata never hid
That's why I want to pull the stunt that Mata Hari did.

Refrain
YOUNG LADIES — Mata Hari, Mata Hari,
Oh, what a wicked girl was she
That's the kind of girl I shouldn't be
Mata Hari, Mata Hari,
That's the kind of wicked girl I shouldn't be.

Interlude
NANCY

Mata's wiles were sinister
Towards a big Prime Minister
Handsome guards were in a stir
 And a king or two
Once inside the castle gate
Mata'd never vacillate
Facile, she would wrestle late
 'Til she got her due
Somehow she would steal the secret documents and then
They would ask her back to steal some documents again.

YOUNG LADIES

When
Mata Hari had a very wicked reputation
She was willing to be thrilling for her information

NANCY

As she died she said "What fun:
 It's the only thing I haven't done!"

NANCY &
YOUNG LADIES

For her the men all had a yen yet Mata never hid
That's why I want to pull the stunt that Mata Hari did

Refrain
NANCY &
YOUNG LADIES

(Dance Interlude)

Mata Hari, Mata Hari
Oh, what a wicked girl was she
That's the kind of girl I want to be
 Mata Hari, Mata Hari,
That's the kind of wicked girl I want to be;
 Mata Hari, Mata Hari
 Oh, what a wicked girl was she
That's the kind of girl I want to be

NANCY &
YOUNG LADIES

Mata Hari, Mata Hari,
 That's the kind of wicked girl I want to be;
Like Mata!
(During the last refrain NANCY climbs out the window. She is on the end of a line of knotted sheets which the YOUNG LADIES have gotten from the bed. NANCY gives a tug on the line and the YOUNG LADIES collapse on the bed at . . .)
BLACKOUT

Act II

SCENE 5

The Primrose Path, with garden bench. ERNESTINE VON LIEBEDICH'S voice is heard as the lights come up. She is discovered doing bending exercises.

ERNESTINE
Eins, zwei, drei, fire. Eins, zwei, drei, fire. Eins, zwei, drei, . . .
 (OSCAR FAIRFAX backs on from L. carrying a pistol. He wheels around and confronts Ernestine)

OSCAR
Good Heavens!

ERNESTINE

(Raising hands over head)

Funf! Don't shoot der gun. I didn't do it.

OSCAR

Oh, do forgive me, Madame. There are still some wild Indians about. How unseemly of me to arrive at such a time.

ERNESTINE

Iss notting; for der exercise it is to me der constant comrade like der breezing. Do you breeze, General Fairfax?

OSCAR

You know my name, Madame? Have we met? No, I am sure I could not have forgotten so fine a face and figure as yours.

ERNESTINE

(Sitting on bench)

Little Mary oft speak of her friend, der General Fairfax und I put zwei und zwei togezer.

OSCAR

Ah, then you, you must be the famous Madame Ernestine von Liebedich.

(ERNESTINE acknowledges this. OSCAR bows low)

Ah, Madame, it is indeed a privilege and an honor to meet you face to face. How well I recall your "Carmen."

ERNESTINE

Vas my favorite role. I vas der first person ever to sing "Carmen" . . . in German.

(Rising and singing unaccompanied)

"Ja, die liebe hat brunte flugel

Solch' einen vogel fangt man schwer."

I premiere it in Vienna. It make me overnight success.

OSCAR

Ah, Vienna.

ERNESTINE

Know you Vienna, General?

OSCAR

Believe it or not, Madame Ernestine, I was once a struggling young painter in Vienna. The family gave me a year to find out I wasn't an artist.

(Sitting on bench)

Actually I found out much sooner, for the only painting I ever sold was one my landlady had hung upside down by mistake. I was forced to change the title from "The Mountain" to "The Valley." Ah, but that was a year: Vienna, 1884.

ERNESTINE

Eighty-four? Dat der very year I come from homeland to study der voice.

OSCAR

You were in Vienna then? I wonder if we could have met.

(Rising)

Did you by any chance frequent the Blue Danube Cafe?

ERNESTINE

I only know from der outside looking in. I very poor den. I spend all money on der voice lessons. Perhaps you go to der lovely free chamber music concerts?

I must confess I wasn't one much for chamber music. Did you spend any time at the Red Stocking?

ERNESTINE

Ock! I vas much too proper young lady for der Red Stocking. Der State Museum?

OSCAR

Much too impetuous for the State Museum. I, I'm sorry we missed each other.

ERNESTINE

Ya, iss pity.
(Music in under dialogue)

ERNESTINE

Yet, Vienna was many tings to many people und each, each have dare own happy memory.
(Sit sits on bench as:)
(ERNESTINE and OSCAR sing DO YOU EVER DREAM OF VIENNA?)

DO YOU EVER DREAM OF VIENNA?
(ERNESTINE and OSCAR)

1st Refrain

ERNESTINE	Do you ever dream of Vienna?
OSCAR	I think I do, I'm sure I do
ERNESTINE	Remember the strudel? So tasty, but dear, . . .
OSCAR	How well I remember: *(Patting paunch)* My one souvenir.
ERNESTINE	The way that we waltzed then How regal; how grand, . . .
OSCAR	The youngsters don't waltz now, . . .
ERNESTINE	They don't understand Do you ever dream of Vienna? . . . Vienna of days gone by.

(Nostalgic waltz music is heard as background to the following dialogue)

OSCAR

(Once again the young swain; bowing low)
May I have the pleasure of this waltz?

ERNESTINE

(Playing the game)
Danke, but der card; it is all filled.

OSCAR

Then I shall fly with you to the balcony where no one shall recognize us.
(He takes her hand and for a few moments they waltz in happy memory. ERNESTINE then stops and turns to him)

2nd Refrain

ERNESTINE	Do you ever dream of Vienna?
OSCAR	Oh, yes, I do I often do

ERNESTINE	I see it so clearly, Through eyes vaguely dim
OSCAR	The Artist,
ERNESTINE	The Singer,
OSCAR	How reckless:
ERNESTINE	How prim! But I first performed there.
OSCAR	My paintings weren't hung:
ERNESTINE	Ah, what does it matter? My dear, . . . we were young:
BOTH	Do you ever dream of Vienna? . . . Vienna of days gone by.

(*OSCAR takes ERNESTINE's hand, kisses it with a flourish at . . .*)
BLACKOUT
ENCORE*
DO YOU EVER DREAM OF VIENNA?
(ERNESTINE and OSCAR)

Encore Refrain

ERNESTINE	Do you ever dream of Vienna?
OSCAR	Oh, yes I do
ERNESTINE	Ya, ya; I too
OSCAR	Did you go that year To the costume affair?
ERNESTINE	The one on the Danube? Oh, yes, I was there; I won second prize So I'll never forget,
OSCAR	But I won the first prize, . . .
BOTH	Thank heaven, we've met! Do you ever dream of Vienna? . . . Vienna of days gone by.

* If the encore is used a fadeout rather than a blackout should be used at the end of the second refrain and ERNESTINE and OSCAR should exit D.R., reentering D.R. for encore. Hand kissing business and blackout should be used at end of encore.

Act II

SCENE 6

Point Look-Out.
Attacca; "A SHELL GAME" — DANCE PANTOMIME:
YELLOW FEATHER, BILLY and NANCY.
(*Music mysterioso in. YELLOW FEATHER gives Indian war cry, (lights up), he is discovered Stage R. YELLOW FEATHER does a mysterious war-dance. BILLY backs on from Stage L. The two turn and pass each other; stop; turn around and come back to look at one another, face to face. BILLY pretends he is YELLOW FEATHER's reflection. YELLOW FEATHER, at first uncertain, tries various poses, which BILLY imitates. Almost satisfied, YEL-*

ACT II SCENE 6 (con't.)

LOW FEATHER starts out L. BILLY thumbs his nose at Yellow Feather. YELLOW FEATHER turns around rapidly and almost catches him. YELLOW FEATHER stares at his "reflection" as NANCY enters L. She throws off her "Mata Hari" cape and we discover that she is dressed identically to Billy and Yellow Feather. NANCY tip toes past YELLOW FEATHER, does a double-take and turns to him. They size each other up. NANCY does reflection business with YELLOW FEATHER. They grapevine R. toward Billy. Upon seeing each other ALL THREE leap into the air. They begin a "Shell Game", intertwining around each other like three peas. BILLY signals NANCY to exit L. with him but in the confusion he takes YELLOW FEATHER's hand and exits with him. Realizing his mistake, he dashes back to NANCY and exits R. with her, followed by YELLOW FEATHER. Off Stage THEY get confused again and BILLY is seen leading YELLOW FEATHER from R. to L. BILLY realizes he has made another mistake and dashes Stage R. YELLOW FEATHER follows as far as C. and stops for he sees NANCY who has crossed to extreme L. backing toward C. and BILLY backing toward C. from R. YELLOW FEATHER stands his ground and waits until THEY bump into him. BILLY and NANCY reach behind themselves and feel their way up YELLOW FEATHER's sides until their hands finally meet at his chest. YELLOW FEATHER tries not to laugh as THEY tickle him. BILLY and NANCY turn in to each other, start to embrace and then realize that YELLOW FEATHER is standing there.

BILLY gives YELLOW FEATHER a polite "Kadota". NANCY takes BILLY's hand and they run off L. YELLOW FEATHER gives a war cry and starts to follow them off as BILLY and NANCY reappear at edge of L. As THEY point off R., BILLY says "They went that-a-way". BILLY and NANCY exit L. as YELLOW FEATHER leaps off R. at

BLACKOUT)

Act II

SCENE 7

The Inn. LITTLE MARY enters R. during Blackout. She carries a small lantern. The follow spot is pin-pointed on her face. XING L., she puts her hand to her mouth and calls:

LITTLE MARY

(Calling softly)
Captain Jim,
(Getting no answer she crosses R. and calls again)
Oh, Captain Jim.
(Her shoulders drop for a moment. A Cuckoo call is heard from stage L. Courage again takes over and she forces a sweet smile to her face as she crosses L.)
(Calling softly)
Coo Coo.
(The CUCKOO BIRD answers back)
Coo Coo.
(The CUCKOO BIRD answers again as . . .)
(Music in, COO COO, sung by LITTLE MARY)
COO COO
(LITTLE MARY)

LITTLE MARY
Introduction   When e'er I'm sad the Coo-coo sings
                                Such happy, carefree words;
                        It seems this little thought he brings,
                                "The world is for the birds"

Refrain   Coo Coo, I love your merry song,
                        Coo Coo, It's like a fairy song,
                        Coo Coo, It can't be very wrong
                                When you coo,
                                "Coo Coo"
                        Coo Coo, So happy in your tree,
                        Coo Coo, How happy you must be,
                        Coo Coo, To sing so merrily;
                                Coo Coo, I'm blue:
                                        You coo your Coo Coo
                                        As all Coo Coos do;
                                        I'll Coo Coo, too,
                        "Coo Coo"!
(At the end of the song LITTLE MARY picks up lantern, places it on porch of Inn. She crosses to tree UR. Dramatically she leans against the tree and takes in the night. YELLOW FEATHER leaps leaps from behind the tree where he has been hidden. LITTLE MARY gasps in horror)

LITTLE MARY
(XING D.R.)
Yellow Feather!

YELLOW FEATHER
(XING to Little Mary)
Me have return. Me keep promise. Yellow Feather always keep promise.
        (LITTLE MARY starts to cross L. but YELLOW FEATHER grabs her wrist)
You no happy see Yellow Feather?

LITTLE MARY
Let me go. Please, let me go.

YELLOW FEATHER
No, Merry Sunshine. Me wait long time. Very long time.

LITTLE MARY
What do you want?
        (Little Mary pushes past him and crosses R)
What *do* you want?

YELLOW FEATHER
(Following her)
Me want you, Merry Sunshine. Me have you, . . . now!
        (YELLOW FEATHER and LITTLE MARY struggle but YELLOW FEATHER overpowers her and forces her against tree, UR. YELLOW FEATHER lashes her to the tree with rope and is about to have his way with her when, from off-stage, we hear CAPTAIN JIM calling to his loved one)
                REPRISE — COLORADO LOVE CALL
                (CAPTAIN JIM & LITTLE MARY)

CAPTAIN JIM
(Off-stage)   You-oo-oo and I
                        Shall live and die
                        Underneath a Colorado sky

— 59 —

LITTLE MARY
(*Returning call*)   You-oo-oo and I
Shall live and die
Underneath a Colorado, . . .

(*CAPTAIN JIM enters from U.L. to dramatic music. YELLOW
FEATHER who is hiding on the porch, leaps from the railing as
LITTLE MARY screams to warn CAPTAIN JIM. Having missed
Captain Jim, YELLOW FEATHER takes out a knife. The TWO
MEN meet and struggle as LITTLE MARY looks on in terror. It
looks as if the fight is going YELLOW FEATHER's way until,
with a final burst of energy, CAPTAIN JIM forces the knife from
his hand. YELLOW FEATHER falls to the ground, then runs
out R.*)

(*The music swells as CAPTAIN JIM turns to Little Mary. He goes
to her and unloosens her bonds. He takes her in his arms and as
THEY move D.C. he sings:*)

CAPTAIN JIM   We must forget the past,
My dearest, I am here at last
Our lives have just begun

LITTLE MARY   It's you that I adore,
My dearest, stay forevermore
And we shall be as one

CAPTAIN JIM   Shall be as one

LITTLE MARY   Shall be as one

BOTH   As one
Now you-oo-oo and I
Shall live and die
Underneath a Colorado sky
Our love today
Shall rule for aye
Shall rule for aye
For aye!

(*CAPTAIN JIM starts to embrace LITTLE MARY as she turns away
and breaks R.*)

LITTLE MARY

Oh, Captain Jim, how thoughtless of me to contemplate our happy life
together when a man's destiny hangs in the balance. Although Yellow
Feather has been most wicked, indeed, still I am grieved, both for him and
his dear father, to think what is in store for such a one.

CAPTAIN JIM

Do not fret, Miss Mary. The Inn has been surrounded by my men and
they have no doubt apprehended Yellow Feather by now. Chief Brown
Bear need never know of the base state into which his son has fallen until
the Forest Rangers have returned him to the world as a useful member of
society.

LITTLE MARY

Oh, Captain Jim, a Forest Ranger is truly a man.

CAPTAIN JIM

Yes, Little Mary, he is.
(*The Forest Ranger music in*)

LITTLE MARY

(Running R. and looking off)

Look, dear Captain. Your brave men return from their noble endeavors.
How proud you must feel and, oh, how happy the young ladies shall be
to hear of their safe return.

*(LITTLE MARY runs to the Inn porch, turns, blows a kiss to Captain
JIM, then exits into the Inn)*

*(The FOREST RANGERS enter from U.R. reprising their song. The
YOUNG LADIES enter from the Inn and a joyous reunion takes
place. As the reprise draws to a close NANCY & BILLY enter
from the Inn followed by ERNESTINE & OSCAR)*

OSCAR

(Crossing to Captain Jim)

Captain Warington?

CAPTAIN JIM

(Saluting)

Yes, Sir?

OSCAR

It is unfortunate that I must ask you to interrupt this joyous reunion but
you and your men must immediately assist me in locating an Indian by
the name of, . . .

(Checking paper)

Chief Brown Bear.

CHIEF BROWN BEAR

(Having entered from U.S.)

How! Me Chief Brown Bear!

OSCAR

Excellent work, Captain! Now then, as Temporary Undersecretary, Second
in Charge of Indian Affairs and by the power invested in me by the
Government of the United States of America, it is my duty to inform you
that our Supreme Court has reached a decision in the suit brought against
my Government by you and the Kadota Tribe. The Court has decided in
your favor. We are therefore returning to you and your people approximately
one quarter of the State of Colorado. Your deed, Sir

CHIEF BROWN BEAR

(Taking deed and turning front)

Justice triumph! Kadota honor restored. Now me give land away. First,
to adopted daughter, Merry Sunshine, me give this ground where stand
Colorado Inn. Now she burn mortgage. All else me give to new adopted
son, Yellow Feather.

(Hands deed to Billy)

BILLY

Gee, dad.

CHIEF BROWN BEAR

Me give in hope he make National Park and Refuge for animal and tree,
so good and noble Forest Ranger have place to call home.

(LITTLE MARY leads FLEET FOOT on from U.L.)

LITTLE MARY

Look, Indian Father, a surprise: your dear old friend, Fleet Foot.

FLEET FOOT

(Embracing OSCAR by mistake)

B.own Bear! Brown Bear, um ton go la! Um ton go la!

CHIEF BROWN BEAR
(Crosses to Fleet Foot, embraces him and leads him Right, saying . . .)
Soo taun cha. Soo taun cha, Fleet Foot.

FLEET FOOT
Um ton go la. Um ton go la, Brown Bear.

LITTLE MARY
(Turns to CAPTAIN JIM and gives him her hands)
Oh, Captain Jim!

CAPTAIN JIM
Little Mary!

OSCAR
(Carried away)
Ernestine!

ERNESTINE
(Surprised)
Oshcar!

NANCY
(It's a question)
Billy?

BILLY
(Raising arm)
How!
(Finale music in as all COUPLES embrace)
FINALE, ACT II
(TUTTI)

TUTTI   When e'er a cloud appears
                 Filled with doubt and fears
                 Look for a sky of blue
                 When e'er a cloud of grey
                 Seems to waft your way
                 Look for a sky of blue
                 Remember, sometimes the sun is shining
                 It may be shining some day for you-oo-oo
                 So 'til that happy day
                 We must learn to say
                 Look to your country, true:
*(It begins to snow as YELLOW FEATHER enters and marches D.C.
He carries a large American flag, waving in the breeze)*

TUTTI   "My country 'tis of thee
                 Sweet land of liberty,"

LITTLE MARY   Look to the Red, White and Blue.
(The entire company wave small American flags as . . .)

THE CURTAIN FALLS

FINALE ULTIMO

(Curtain Calls)

— 62 —

TUTTI

(TUTTI)

You've got to hand it to Little Mary Sunshine
Little Mary is the sunshine of the sun;
You've got to hand it to Little Mary Sunshine:
Little Mary has a smile for everyone;
She may be a bit old fashioned, but then,
When you unlock your heart, sublime,
You've got to hand it to Little Mary Sunshine
For she's very merry at all time.

THE CURTAIN FALLS

CURTAIN CALLS

(The curtain rises on the ENSEMBLE for bows. PETE points D.R. and FLEET FOOT comes to C. from D.R. After bow, he points to D.L. for YELLOW FEATHER. YELLOW FEATHER comes to C. for bow then points to D.R. for CHIEF BROWN BEAR's bow and so on to OSCAR, to BILLY, to CAPTAIN JIM, to ERNESTINE, to NANCY. The entire company then spreads to make room for LITTLE MARY. LITTLE MARY, flowers in her arms, comes to D.C. from U.L. She bows as the curtain falls. Curtain up. LITTLE MARY steps to pit and throws a rose to the CONDUCTOR. As she steps back into place the curtain falls. Curtain up. Full Company bow as:)

THE CURTAIN FALLS

Other Publications for Your Interest